若松丈太郎 英日詩集
Jotaro Wakamatsu
A Collection of Poems in English and Japanese

かなしみの土地
Land of Sorrow

与那覇恵子／郡山 直 翻訳
Translated by
Keiko Yonaha, Naoshi Koriyama

メーガン・クックルマン 監修
Translation was supervised by Meghan Kuckelman

コールサック社
Coal Sack Publishing Company

若松丈太郎英日詩集　かなしみの土地　目次

序文に代えて　極端粘り族の誇りと希望　鈴木比佐雄　6

Ⅰ章　若松丈太郎のウクライナ・福島の原発詩篇

かなしみの土地

若松丈太郎英日詩集　かなしみの土地

序文に代えて　極端粘り族の誇りと希望

鈴木比佐雄

若松丈太郎の詩篇を今も困難な状況の中で生きるウクライナ人やウクライナに心を寄せる日本や世界の人びとに届けたいと願って、この英日詩集『かなしみの土地』を企画・刊行した。

若松氏の奥様の若松蓉子氏は、この趣旨に賛同し出版のご承諾を下さり、背中を押して下さった。また英語に翻訳してくれた与那覇恵子氏と郡山直氏、その監修をされたメーガン・クックルマン氏たちの労力にも心から感謝を申し上げたい。

遠からずこの詩選集がウクライナ語にも翻訳されることの可能性も探っていきたい。

若松氏が亡くなった二〇二一年四月の翌月に、私は追悼詩を文芸誌「コールサック」に掲載したが、左記には序文に代えて、その詩を再録したい。

極端粘り族の誇りと希望
──若松丈太郎氏追悼

東電福島第一原発から二〇㎞の立入禁止区域検問所
多くの車両が拒絶されて引き返していった

6

あなたが「埴谷・島尾記念文学資料館調査員」の名刺を
差し出し二言三言話すと警察官たちは通してくれた
名刺が魔法のチケットのように思えて
「かなしみの土地」である小高・浪江への門が開かれた

十年前の二〇一一年四月十日の小高駅前商店街は
あなたの予言した「神隠しされた街」になっていた
曇り空でたわんだ電線に鴉だけが舞っていた

駅前通りに並ぶ百件ほどの商店の中に薬局店があった
「この薬局は誰の実家か知っていますか？」
答えられずにいると
「日本国憲法に影響を与えた鈴木安蔵の実家ですよ」
と誇らしげに伝えて少し頬をゆるめた

生まれ育った岩手県奥州市岩谷堂の商店街と重ねながら
一万人の暮らす小高の街の人びとの文芸の歴史を語り始め
あなたの眼差しこそが「核発電」事故による「核災」から

立ち上がる人びとの背中を押す希望そのものだった

十年後の二〇二一年五月三日に私はその場所に立った
その薬局は看板も店も裏の大きな蔵も無くなっていた
あなたが愛した商店街は歯抜けになりながらも
銀行の支店や営業を再開した店も出てきた

昨日は南相馬市内のメモリアルホールであなたを偲ぶ会があった
二人の息子真樹さんと央樹さんが父を畏敬し誇りに思う言葉
妻の蓉子さんの夫に寄り添い支えたことへの誇りの言葉
管理職にならずに一教師として悩める子どもの言葉に耳を傾け
地元の手作りの文化活動や表現者たちを慈しみ
草の根の原発廃止運動の人びとの思想の核となったあなたは
詩と評論の言葉で全国の人びとの背骨のような存在だった

教師を退いたあなたは一九九四年にチェルノブイリに行き
連作「かなしみの土地　6　神隠しされた街」を書き上げた
また浮舟文化会館「埴谷・島尾記念文学資料館」調査員になり

埴谷雄高に会いに行き島尾敏雄の妻ミホを訪ね

貴重な資料を文学資料館に寄贈してもらった

あなたが長年研究していた福島浜通りの文学史は

『極端粘り族の系譜――相馬地方と近現代文学とその周辺』として

すでに編集を終え原稿もほぼまとまっている

あなたの言葉こそが誰よりも「極端粘り族」であったことを

あなたの言葉こそが福島浜通りの「誇りと希望」であったと

この書物や多くの詩篇が語り継いでいくだろう

Ⅰ章　若松丈太郎のウクライナ・福島の原発詩篇

かなしみの土地

わたしたちは世代を超えて苦しむことになるでしょう

—— ウクライナ医学アカデミー放射線科学臨床医療研究所所長
ウラディミール・ロマネンコ

プロローグ　ヨハネ黙示録

その日と
その日につづく日々について
聖ヨハネは次のように予言した

たいまつのように燃えた大きな星が空から落ちてきた。
星は川の三分の一とその水源との上に落ちた。
星の名はニガヨモギと言って、
水の三分の一がニガヨモギのように苦くなった。
水が苦くなったため多くの人びとが死んだ。*1

チェルノブイリ国際学術調査センター主任
ウラディミール・シェロシタンは

かなしい町であるチェルノブイリへようこそ！
と私たちへの挨拶をはじめた
ニガヨモギを意味する東スラヴのことばで
名づけられたこの土地は
名づけられたときからかなしみの土地であったのか
一九八六年四月二十六日
チェルノブイリ原子力発電所四号炉爆発
この日と
この日につづく日々
多くの人びとが死に
多くの人びとが苦しんでいる　さらに
多くの人びとが苦しみつづけねばならない

1　百年まえの蝶

きょうの未明に自死した二十五歳の青年がいる
離陸して高度をあげるエアバスA－310の窓外に眼をやる

百年まえのそのことを思いつつ

つきぬけた雲海のうえ

ふと一羽の蝶が舞っていたと見たのは幻にちがいないが

　こたびは別れて西ひがし、

　振りかへりつゝ、去りにけり。*2

一八九四年五月十六日未明の二十五歳の青年の思いと

一九九四年五月十六日そのことを思う者の思いと

に架けるものはあるか

あれば何か

あれは何か

あれは蝶ではないか

エアバスの窓外に

もつれあい舞う

幻

14

2　五月のキエフに

古い石造りの街のなかぞらを綿毛がさすらっている
ポプラの綿毛だ
白い花をつけたマロニエ並木は石造りの街なみに似つかわしい
キエフはヨーロッパでもっとも緑に富む都市だという

五月のフレシャーチク通りを人びとは楽しんでいる
五月の夜を人びとは並木の下のベンチで語らい
人びとは並木の下の散歩道をゆったりと歩んでいる
起伏の多い道は住む人びとのこころの屈折を語っているか

坂道の底にロシア正教寺院が幻境のように現れたりする
私たちは人びとにたちまじって幻境をさすらう
夜のドニエプル川を見ようと街を

ムソルグスキイの「キエフの門」[*3]をたずね
ウクライナの人びとが誇る詩人の名まえを私は記憶した

15

マロニエはシェフチェンコに捧げる花か

3　風景を断ちきるもの

国境警備員が電話で問い合わせている
私たちのマイクロバスはエンジンを止めた
ガイドのヴァーヤさんが書類を置き忘れて来たのだ
空気を抜かれたような静けさである
バスのそとで息を抜こうとする私たちは
バスの近くにいることを指示される
ありふれた一本の道が遮断されて国境である
ベラルーシとウクライナとを分ける
この道の先も後ろも一九九一年までは
ソヴィエト連邦のうちがわであって
人びとは自由に往来していた
道のうえに線がひかれているわけではないが
ありふれた一本のポールで遮断されて国境である

16

国境の道のうえに線がひかれているわけではないが

国境の道のうえに線がひかれているつもりで

私は片脚立ちする

飛び立とうとするこうのとりの片脚立ちの姿を

テオ・アンゲロプロスの映画の一シーンをまねて

ギリシャ・アルバニア・ユーゴスラヴィア国境地帯の

川や湖の多い映画のなかの風景と

ウクライナ・ベラルーシ国境地帯の

目前にひろがるドニエプル川支流の低地との

あまりの相似

けげんな表情で私を見る国境警備員

片脚立ちの姿から私は飛び立つことができようか

こうのとり、たちずさんで*4

こうのとりの巣は農家の軒先の電柱のてっぺんに

あぶなっかしく営まれていたりする

そんな風景のなかで

ウクライナ・ベラルーシ国境がＣ字状に接していて

ありふれた一本の道が¢字状に貫いている

ありふれた一本の道の一〇kmたらずのベラルーシ領

それぞれの国境で出入国審査がある

私たちは境界をつくる

山の尾根に

川の中州に

湖の小島に

林をよぎって畑をよぎって

町のなかを

ブランデンブルク門のまえ

ヴィム・ヴェンダースの天使が国境を越えると*5

モノクロ画面はカラーにかわった

こちら側とあちら側というように

私たちが地図のうえにひいた境界は

私たちのこころにもつながっていて

私たちを差別する

私たちを難民にする

私たちを狙撃する

私たちが国境で足止めされているあいだに

牛乳缶を積んだ小型トラックが
ウクライナからベラルーシへと国境を越えていった
こともなげに
空中の放射性物質も
風にのって
幻蝶のように

　　　4　蘇生する悪霊

目前に
写真で見なれた
チェルノブイリ原子力発電所四号炉
《石棺》
悪しき形相で
まがまがしく
コンクリート五〇万㎥と
鉄材六〇〇〇tとで

封じた冥王プルートの悪霊
その悪霊が蘇生
しそうだという今にも
はげしく反応する線量計
悪霊の気
計測不能
「五分間だけ」
と案内人だが
アスファルト広場
石棺観光用展望台
ではなく焼香台
足もとに埋葬されている汚染物質
五分とここにいたくはない
痛くはないが
私たちは冒されている
冒された鉄骨の残骸
赤錆荒々しく
剥離する

野ざらし
風すぎて
ここは荒涼
冒された森林
時ならぬ紅葉であったと
《ニンジン色の森》
人びとの不安の形象
伐採され
埋葬され
周辺に森林なく
ここは満目蕭条

5　《死》に身を曝す

　チェルノブイリ三〇kmゾーンの境界にゲートがある。ゲート脇から立入禁止区域を限る鉄線を張った粗末な柵が延々とつづいている。ここまでは緑うつくしい穀物畑が視野いっぱいに広がっていたが、柵の内側は荒れるにまかせた畑に赤枯れた草が所在なげに立ちつくしてい

る。私たちが迎えを待つあいだに、キエフ方面から三台のバスがやってきた。乗って来た人たちは別のバスに乗り換える。汚染されていないバスと汚染されているバスとをゲートを境に別にしているのだろう。さまざまな年齢の彼ら彼女らはチェルノブイリ原子力発電所で働いている人たちである。発電所やその関連施設で二週間勤務してはチェルノブイリ原子力発電所で働いている人たちである。発電所やその関連施設で二週間勤務しては交替するのだという。三〇㎞ゾーンは立入禁止がたてまえだが、想像以上に多くの人たちが生活しているらしい。事故のあった四号炉に隣接する一〜三号炉は稼働しているし、私たちが説明を受け、昼食をとった国際学術調査センターもゾーンの内側にある。ほかにも研究施設などがあるとのことだ。バスで五、六号炉近くを通りかかったとき、人工池で釣りをしている人たちを見かけた。昼休みの気ばらしだというが、まさか釣った魚を食べることはあるまいと思うものの、おそらく汚染されているにちがいない人工池で平気で遊んでいる様子におどろいてしまった。四号炉の《展望台》では持参した線量計のカウンターが振り切れてしまい、私たちが浮き足立っているのに、すぐそばを作業員たちが日常的なこととして通り過ぎて行く。ゾーンのなかをバスに同乗して案内してくれたのは未婚の若い女性であった。将来の出産を考えれば働くべきところではないと思うのだが、そのことはわきまえていて勤務しているのだそうだ。バスの車窓からは、廃屋となってしまった農家、家畜舎、徒長した果樹の枝、いつものものなのか畑の取り付け道路に刻まれているトラクターの轍などが見え、こころ傷む情景であった。強制退去させられた農民のなかには村に戻って暮らしている人たちが老人を中心にいて、なかば黙認されている。三百五十家族が住んでいたパールシェフ村の人たちも退去させられたが、戻って

きたのはもっとも多いときで百七十人、今は百九人が暮らしているという。七十八歳のマーリア・プーリカさんもそのひとりである。事故のまえに夫と死別し、避難したときはアパートのようなところに酒飲みの男二人と同居させられた。がまんできず三カ月後に戻ってきた。自分は老人なので死ぬのはこわくないと私たちに語った。事が起こると普通の生活を維持できなくなるのが普通の人たちである。普通の人たちが生きるためには《死》に身を曝さねばならない。

6　神隠しされた街

四万五千の人びとが二時間のあいだに消えた
サッカーゲームが終わって競技場から立ち去った
のではない
人びとの暮らしがひとつの都市からそっくり消えたのだ
ラジオで避難警報があって
「三日分の食料を準備してください」
多くの人は三日たてば帰れると思って
ちいさな手提げ袋をもって

なかには仔猫だけをだいた老婆も
入院加療中の病人も
千百台のバスに乗って
四万五千の人びとが二時間のあいだに消えた
鬼ごっこする子どもたちの歓声が
隣人との垣根ごしのあいさつが
郵便配達夫の自転車のベル音が
ボルシチを煮るにおいが
家々の窓の夜のあかりが
人びとの暮らしが
地図のうえからプリピャチ市が消えた
チェルノブイリ事故発生四〇時間後のことである
千百台のバスに乗って
プリピャチ市民が二時間のあいだにちりぢりに
近隣三村をあわせて四万九千人が消えた
四万九千人といえば
私の住む原町市の人口にひとしい
さらに

原子力発電所中心半径三〇kmゾーンは危険地帯とされ

十一日目の五月六日から三日のあいだに九万二千人が

あわせて約十五万人

人びとは一〇〇kmや一五〇km先の農村にちりぢりに消えた

半径三〇kmゾーンといえば

東京電力福島第一原子力発電所を中心に据えると

双葉町

大熊町

富岡町

楢葉町

浪江町

広野町

川内村

都路村

葛尾村

小高町　いわき市北部

そして私の住む原町市がふくまれる

こちらもあわせて約十五万人

私たちが消えるべき先はどこか

私たちはどこに姿を消せばいいのか

事故六年のちに避難命令が出た村さえもある

事故八年のちの旧プリピャチ市に

私たちは入った

亀裂がはいったペーヴメントの

亀裂をひろげて雑草がたけだけしい
ツバメが飛んでいる
ハトが胸をふくらませている
チョウが草花に羽をやすめている
ハエがおちつきなく動いている
蚊柱が回転している
街路樹の葉が風に身をゆだねている
それなのに

人声のしない都市
人の歩いていない都市
四万五千の人びとがかくれんぼしている都市
鬼の私は捜しまわる

幼稚園のホールに投げ捨てられた玩具
台所のこんろにかけられたシチュー鍋
オフィスの机上のひろげたままの書類
ついさっきまで人がいた気配はどこにもあるのに
日がもう暮れる
鬼の私はとほうに暮れる

友だちがみんな神隠しにあってしまって
私は広場にひとり立ちつくす
デパートもホテルも
文化会館も学校も
集合住宅も
崩れはじめている
すべてはほろびへと向かう
人びとのいのちと
人びとがつくった都市と
ほろびをきそいあう
ストロンチウム九〇　半減期　二九年
セシウム一三七　　　半減期　三〇年
プルトニウム二三九　半減期二四〇〇〇年
セシウムの放射線量が八分の一に減るまでに九〇年
致死量八倍のセシウムは九〇年後も生きものを殺しつづける
人は百年後のことに自分の手を下せないということであれば
人がプルトニウムを扱うのは不遜というべきか
捨てられた幼稚園の広場を歩く

雑草に踏み入れる

雑草に付着していた核種が舞いあがったにちがいない

肺は核種のまじった空気をとりこんだにちがいない

神隠しの街は地上にいっそうふえるにちがいない

私たちの神隠しはきょうかもしれない

うしろで子どもの声がした気がする

ふりむいてもだれもいない

なにかが背筋をぞくっと襲う

広場にひとり立ちつくす

7　囚われ人たち

　キエフ小児科・産婦人科研究所の病院に入院している子どもたちに会って、ウクライナとベラルーシの子どもたちは囚われ人なのではあるまいかという思いをいだいた。医師と異国人とが通訳を介して自分たちを話題にしているその片言隻句のなかから、自分の貶められている不条理な状況についての情報を読みとろうと、子どもたちは注意力を集中している様子であった。

　子どもたちはおとなが思い込んでいるよりはるかに真実の核心にせまって正しい理解に達して

28

いるものである。私は子どもたちのそんな様子を見ながら、半世紀まえのフリョーラとグラー

シャのことを思い出していた。ふたりは、一九四三年にドニエプル川の上流であるベラルーシ

の小さな村でおこなわれたナチスの犯罪を告発した映画「炎／628」のなかの少年と少女で

ある。かつて私はこのフリョーラとグラーシャのことにふれて「冬に」という詩を書いた。

冬に*7

北へ十二月下旬

枯れがれの雑木林

定着液にどっぷりつかった風景

そこひを病んでいる想像力

動き出そうとするものはないのか

小さな途中駅で

左脚をわずかにひきずる娘が乗車した

ぼくのまえの座席に腰をおろした娘は頬骨がやや張って

グラーシャに似ている

眼のあたりや唇も

白い笛をくわえたグラーシャは内腿を

血に染めて丘を下って来る
フリョーラのまえに脚をひきずって来る
フリョーラの眼は人間の歴史と世界の全体とを見すぎてしまって
白ロシア共和国ハトィニ村一九四三年にいて少年とは思えない皺を顔に刻んだ
一九四五年からほんとうに信じていいものをなくしてしまった
のではないかぼくも

行き場を失って吹き寄せられたように
街角に若者たちが群がっている

ぼくは詩集を一冊買った
ハトィニ村は一九八六年四月チェルノブイリの風下ではなかったのか
夜　新しい年のカレンダーを床にひろげルーペで人の姿を捜す
一月サンモリッツ　人の姿なし
二月ルツェルン　人影なし
何月に人に逢えるのか
三月ツェルマット　いない
四月モントール　うずくまっている人の姿があるようにも見える
ルマン湖の桟橋に

映画のなかの表情だからそれはつくられたものであることは承知したうえで、フリョーラの表情を私は忘れることはない。この世紀ほど子どもに対してむごい仕打ちをし、しつづけている時代は過去になかったにちがいない。それもこの世紀のほぼ後半のことだ。無差別爆撃、核爆弾の投下、強制収容所での虐殺は言うまでもない。日々のくらしの裂け目に陰湿な露頭を見せる。この世紀はつぎの世紀を生きる子どもたちに何を寄託しようとしているのだろう。ウクライナ医学アカデミー付属キエフ小児科・産婦人科研究所の病院にいる子どもたちに会いながら、すべての子どもたちは囚われ人なのではあるまいかという思いに至った。

8　苦い水の流れ

冬ふりつもった雪を融かし
天からの恵みの水を集め
五月のドニエプル川の支流は
自然堤防を越え
ふくらみあふれ
見渡すかぎりは田植えられたばかりの水田のように
たっぷりと水を湛えている

沃土が熟成されている

広大なドニエプル川の流域

ウクライナだけではなく

ロシアやベラルーシもその水源にして

プリピャチ川が合流するあたりに

チェルノブイリがある

上流から三分の一のあたり

セシウム一三七による汚染地図をひろげると

上流三分の一地域が彩色されていて

苦い水を川におし流している

チェルノブイリ一〇kmゾーン内の

ニガヨモギが茂る土饅頭の下に

八百の土饅頭の下に汚染物質が葬られている

八百の土饅頭が地下水を苦い水にかえている

《石棺》がひびわれはじめたと

熱と重みによって地盤の状態は危機的だと

発電所の人工池から水はプリピャチ川に流れ

プリピャチ川はドニエプル川に流れ

ゆたかなドニエプル川は苦い水を内蔵して流れゆく

9　白夜にねむる水惑星

厚い水蒸気膜にくるまれて
水惑星は眼下に沈んでいる
東に向けての孤独な飛行
モスクワ午後八時離陸の旅客機は
太陽を左手に定め
時を停め
浮遊しているかのようだ
ここは白夜で
夕陽はそのまま朝の光を放ちはじめる
よどんだ夜の地表を
川は流れつづけているだろう
一日のはじまりをまえに
人びとは不安なつかのまのねむりに沈んでいるだろう

夢のなか蝶は舞っているだろうか
窓外に蝶はいない

エピローグ　かなしみのかたち
東京国立博物館で国宝法隆寺展をみる

日光菩薩像をまえ
に　ウクライナの子どもたちを思った
いまさらのように気づいた
ひとのかなしみは千年まえ
も　いまも変わりないのだ
そして過去にあった
ものは　将来にも予定されてあるのだ
あふれるなみだ
あふれるドニエプルの川づら
あふれる苦い水

注 この連詩は、一九九四年五月十六日から二十日までのあいだチェルノブイリ福島県民調査団に参加して得たものである。

*1 「ヨハネ黙示録」第八章10、11。ただし、原意をそこなわない程度に語句の一部を改変した。

*2 北村透谷「雙蝶のわかれ」部分。《透谷全集》第一巻)

*3 ムソルグスキイ「展覧会の絵」のなかの曲名。

*4 テオ・アンゲロプロス監督作品「こうのとり、たちずさんで」(一九九一年・ギリシャ)

*5 ヴィム・ヴェンダース監督作品「ベルリン・天使の詩」(一九八八年・西ドイツ・フランス)

*6 エレム・クリモフ監督作品「炎/628」(一九八五年・ソ連)

*7 『88福島県現代詩集』初出。

参照したおもな図書
・松岡信夫『ドキュメント　チェルノブイリ』(一九八八年・緑風出版)
・広河隆一『チェルノブイリ報告』(一九九一年・岩波新書)
・アラ・ヤロシンスカヤ『チェルノブイリ極秘』(一九九四年・平凡社)

（編註）
詩集『いくつもの川があって』では、「プロローグ　ヨハネ黙示録」が「1　ヨハネ黙示録」と改題され、「1　百年まえの蝶」及び「エピローグ　かなしみのかたち」は収録されなかった。本書では、初出となる、アンソロジー『悲歌』(一九九四年、銅林社)所収の「かなしみの土地」を載録した。なお、『若松丈太郎詩選集一三〇篇』(二〇一四年、コールサック社)にもこのオリジナルバージョンが収録されている。

35

いくつもの川があって

夜のドニエプル川を見よう
街灯の暗い坂道をのぼったり
街灯のすくない坂道をくだったり
忽然浮かぶアンドレイ教会
教会のあたりから黄泉の夜道へさまよい歩く
さまよいましょう
ウラジーミルの丘をさまよったのか
ピオネール公園をさまよったのか
黄泉の夜道をさまようほどに
ドニエプル川はいっそう遠のく
見えないドニエプル川は川幅を増し
見えないドニエプル川は水かさを増し
黒ぐろといっさいをのみこんで

36

わたしはのみこまれ

胎内めぐりに身を任す

さまよいましょう

夜の川を見ようという気になったのはなぜ

川岸への道を見つけてさえいたら

暗い川面を漂い流れるわたしに出会えたか

al Berkah（祝福）の間の壁面に映る

al Beerkah（貯水池）の中庭の池の波がつくる光と影

アルハンブラ宮殿の壁面に映る光と影の揺らめきをぼんやり眺めていると、四十歳ほどの男が「日本人ですか」と話しかけてきた。聞くと、フィンランドでの生活が二十年になること、土地の女性と結婚していることを話し、「あれと一緒です」と、やや離れたところにいる女性を示す。妻がおととし、フィンランドとバルト三国を旅行し、いたく気に入って帰ってきたことを言うと、「それはよかったですね」と応じた。とりとめのない日本語の破片があたりに散らばった。その破片に木漏れ日が注いだり、影が落ちたり。

37

立ち去ってゆく男の姿に哀愁のようなものを感じたと言えば、でき過ぎか。

al Beerkah の水がつくる光と影が
al Berkah の壁に映ると
〝e〟がひとつどこかへ隠れてしまう
隠れてしまったのは　〝e〟の音だけ？
男もフィンランド人の妻とともに al Berkah の壁の陰に　隠れてしまった
al Berkah の壁に映る光と陰
その揺らめきをぼんやり眺めている

五月のヨーロッパをポプラの綿毛が飛んでいる
ウクライナ平原の空から
クラコフやプラハのほうへ
ベオグラードやサラエヴォのほうへ
ちいさな種子をはこんで
夏の雪が飛んでいる
地雷が仕掛けられた地球

地雷原をポプラの綿毛が飛んでいる

五月の地球にちいさな種子をはこんで

気まぐれに放射性物質もはこんで

地雷が爆発するとき地球は自爆するかのよう

ドナウ川流域を旅していた一九九九年三月、二十四日はブラチスラヴァに滞在していた。

その夜、五百キロ離れたベオグラードをNATO軍が空爆した。翌二十五日朝のテレビから"EUROPE IN WAR"という文字が目にとびこんできた。この日、スロヴァキアのコマルノから国境のドナウ川を越えて、ハンガリー側のコマロムへ入国するとき、きびしい警備がおこなわれていて、特に個人旅行者への対応が通常より厳重だということだった。一方で、土地の人たちは国境の橋を徒歩や自転車、乗用車などで普段どおりに往来している様子だ。国を別にしてはいるがコマルノとコマロムとはドナウ川をはさんだ隣町という関係である。それが、二十七日にハンガリー側のショプロンとオーストリア側のクリンゲンバッハとのあいだではいっそう厳重で、国境警備員がバスに乗り込みひとりひとりの顔とパスポートの写真とをしげしげと見くらべて照合し、トランクルームも開けて検査するのだった。ヨーロッパの国境は緊張していた。二十六日、ブダペシュトの地下鉄駅でマジャール語の新聞を手に入れた。トップ記事の見出しは"A NATO Kitartóan bombáz"とあった。Belgrád, Küld, Jugoszláviába, Milosevic, などの固有名詞や bombázták といったこと

ばを目で拾うだけだが、状況を読みとろうとつとめる。ブダペシュトはベオグラードから三百キロだ。二十八日午後、ウィーンのヘルデン広場ではセルビア人たちが反NATOの集会をしていた。夜九時になろうとする時刻、シュテファン大寺院まえからケルントナー通りをデモ行進している彼らにふたたび出会った。市電21番から降りると、黒ぐろといっさいをのみこんで流れるドナウ本流に面したホテルに戻るため、が血に染まった不吉な色でつよい光を放っていた。ドナウ川はこのウィーンから、旅をしてきたブラチスラヴァ、ドナウ・ベント、ブダペシュトへと流れ、さらに下ってベオグラードに至るのだ。そこでは今夜も空爆が続いているはずである。

ウミサボテンは触れられると緑色に発光する
ホタルイカももちろんホタルも
発光する生きものはうつくしくかなしい
発光する地球も

夕暮れがた
トゥル　トゥル　トゥルと電話があって
和合さんかな　ちがうな
三十年まえの友だちの声が聞こえてくる

え? ノンちゃん?
ノンちゃんなの?

ヴェランダの支柱の穴をモズが巣にしている
雛鳥がいるらしくひっきりなしに出入りしている
タンポポの綿毛がひっきりなしに飛んでいる
隣家の孫が大きな声を出している
脳腫瘍を手術した母親の世話をしに娘が子連れで里帰りしている
きのうは湿度が高かった
今日の空気は乾燥してひんやりする

ヘレス・デ・ラ・フロンテーラは
水と影、影と水。
なんてロルカが言ってたっけ

FEDERICO GARCIA LORCA のそれぞれの名前のなかに〝RC〟を隠しているのを知ってる?
ロルカはもちろん知ってたはず
ロルカにとっての〝RC〟とはなんだったろう

世界にとっての　"RC"　とはなんだったろう
ロルカが殺されたオリーヴ畑はどこ？
ロルカの死体が隠されたオリーヴ畑はどこ？

石ころだらけのオリーヴ畑のなかをバスが行く
草が生えていない礫土
地球には草も生えない礫土が多い
そんな風景の底から
水音が聞こえて来はしないか
せせらぎと聞こえたのは幻聴か
ひとの話し声と聞こえたのは幻聴か
地球には草も生えない礫土が多い

そんな風景の稜線で断ち切られたむこうから
はじめは布包み
つづいて布包みを載せた頭
そして布包みを頭に載せたひとの上半身
やがて布包みを頭に載せたひとが全身をあらわし

家財のいっさいを頭に載せたひとがたったひとり
ゆっくり近づいてくるのだった
その背後に見えない数万のひとびとが目的地も定めずに　歩きつづけている
わたしは道端に座りこんで
ただ眺めているしかできない
目的地も定めずに歩きつづけているひとびとを
地球には草も生えない礫土が多い
そんな礫土にひとの血が染みこんでいる

雪が降り敷いたその町は傾斜地にあって、一本道のいちばん高い場所からはじめて町全体を眺めたとき、ここに住んでここで死んだ男にわたしは待たれ続けていたことを理解した。
男は店先に椅子を出して座り、待った。坂道のいちばん高い場所に姿をあらわしたわたしが坂道をゆっくり下ってきて男に気づき声をかけるのを、男は待って、椅子に座ったまま一日を過ごした。
その一日が何年も続いた。
その何年ものあいだ、坂道のいちばん高い場所にわたしが立ち、そこから坂道をゆっくり下って男に近づき声をかけることはなかった。

男は死んだ。
男の葬式の日、一本道の町に雪が降り敷いていた。
白い坂道のいちばん高い場所にわたしははじめて立った。
わたしはこの白い町に遅れてきたことを理解した。

なにがあって
なにがなかったの？
そして
これから
なにがあるの？

なにをして
なにをしなかったの？
そして
これから
なにをするの？

海のほうで

トゥル　トゥル　トゥルと電話が鳴っている
だれを呼んでいるのだろう

泥と水
視界のかぎり
気圏の高みから俯瞰する河口の沖積州
茫茫の果てまで
ただ泥と水

茫茫の果てまで
泥と水のほか
存在するものの気配なく
はじまりの世界か
終わりの世界か
静まりかえって
ただ泥と水

はるか上流にバグマティ川と名付けられた支流があって、その河畔にパシュパティナー

ト寺がある。ヒンドゥ教徒は、水辺のガートで朝に沐浴し、昼に洗濯し、アスマサーンで夕べに荼毘（だび）にふされる。バグマティ川はヒンドゥ教徒の骨灰、からだの汚れ、排泄物、そして生きたことのいっさいを川下へ運び流す。そのまた上流の岸辺にラマ教徒のタルチョーが風にはためいている。多くの支流を集めて、ガンガーと呼ばれる大河のほとりはさまざまな人であふれている。仏教徒が香を焚いている。キリスト教徒が聖餐を受けている。イスラム教徒が経典を朗唱している。人びとの骨灰やからだの汚れ、排泄物、そして生きたことのいっさいを併せ呑みこんで、ガンガーは河口の沖積州へと運ぶ。

バグマティ川の浅瀬に
パシュパティナート寺の火葬場
荼毘の炎と煙は空に
骨と灰とは
バグマティ川の浅い流れのなかに燃えさしの薪がひっかかっている
川の瀬も鳴る成瀬川
またの名前を人首川
V字谷を遡って
母の里　米里村人首

ひとかべ

わが幻のハイマート

鬼首という地名もあるのだから

人首があって不思議はない

人首から姥石峠を越え

黄泉の夜道をさまようほどに

尾崎

脚岬

首崎

行きつく先は

死骨崎

さまようものも漂着するか！

あらゆるものがうち揚げられて

なにがあって

なにがなかったの？

混沌たる泥と水

混沌たる泥と水
ただなかに身を沈める
感応してくるものはないか

泥と水のなか
わたしは分解される
わたしのなかに
泥と水が浸透してくる
わたしは泥と水になる
泥と水になったわたしは
産みだせるか
なにかを

渺渺たる水
光をはじいてかがやく
渺渺たる泥
光をはらんでかがやく

光と影
水と影
影と水
泥と水

トゥル　トゥル　トゥルとどこかのだれかの電話がふるえている
受けとるひとのいない電話は空気をいつまでもふるわしつづけている

「かなしみの土地」で「囚われた人たち」に想いを寄せた人

―― 「かなしみの土地」十一篇の読解

鈴木比佐雄

1

『若松丈太郎著作集　全三巻』が若松氏の一周忌の前月に当たる二〇二二年三月初めに刊行された。若松氏の詩篇の最も知られている詩「神隠しされた街」は、連作「かなしみの土地」十一篇の中の「6　神隠しされた街」なのだが、その一篇以外の十篇は私が知る限りでは今まで論じられることが少なく、十一篇の全体像やその連作に貫かれた試みを伝えることは、私が知る限りほとんどなかったように思われる。若松氏を論ずる時に、この連作「かなしみの土地」についていつかその試みと対話してみたいと願っていた。この詩篇群を読み取ることが、若松氏の詩人としての本質的な課題を伝えることになると考えていたからだ。

ところでロシア軍が二〇二二年二月二十四日にウクライナに侵略し数多くの民衆の虐殺を行いながら、チェルノブイリ原子力発電所も占拠し、いまだ放射能物質で汚染されている「赤い森」にも塹壕を築き、キエフに向かっているというニュースが世界を震撼させた。一九九四年四月にこの地を訪ね二〇二一年四月に亡くなった若松丈太郎氏が聞いたならば、どんな見解を明らかにしただろうかと思いを馳せていた。その後、五月にはウクライナ軍がキエフへの攻撃を耐えしのぎ反撃に転じて、ロシア軍もチェルノブイリ原子力発電所から撤退した。そのような情況の中で

日本国内のウクライナ語の表記の仕方がロシア語読みではなく、「チェルノブイリ」が「チョルノービリ」に「キエフ」が「キーウ」になったと報道された。これも若松氏が聞いたならどんな思いを抱いて新しい論考・エッセイを書き綴ったろうか。そんな若松氏の新しい論考などを読むことが出来ないことは、とても残念なことであり、若松氏という世界の悲劇を語りうる詩人・評論家の存在が実は掛け替えのない存在であったことの喪失感が、さらに増して来るのだった。

連作「かなしみの土地」十一篇の各篇は、若松氏に影響を与えた書籍や人物や映画などを記してその試みを掘り下げていき、「チェルノブイリ」（チョルノービリ）という地名が背負った「かなしみの土地」の宿命を物語っていく交響曲のような連作詩篇だと思われる。

若松氏は「プロローグ ヨハネの黙示録」の聖書第八章10、11の原意を損なわないように次のように文意を整えて記している。

《聖ヨハネは次のように予言した／たいまつのように燃えた大きな星が空から落ちてきた。／星は川の三分の一とその水源との上に落ちた。／星の名はニガヨモギと言って、／水の三分の一がニガヨモギのように苦くなった。／水が苦くなったため多くの人びとが死んだ》

若松氏はなぜ聖ヨハネの「たいまつのように燃えた大きな星が空から落ちてきた」という予言の言葉から始めたのか。原発事故とは核爆発であり、それは「燃えた大きな星」が地上に降り注いだようなものである。その「チェルノブイリ」の意味が「ニガヨモギ」であることは、偶然とは言えないこの地が呪われた場所であることを暗示している。

《チェルノブイリ国際学術調査センター主任／ウラディミール・シェロシタンは／かなしい町

であるチェルノブイリへようこそ！／と私たちへの挨拶をはじめた／ニガヨモギを意味する東スラヴのことばで／名づけられたこの土地は／名づけられたときからかなしみの土地であったのか》

ウラディミール・シェロシタン氏の「かなしい町であるチェルノブイリへようこそ！」という言葉が、若松氏の胸中に刻まれて、この時点で「かなしい町」という言葉の意味や響きによって触発されて、連作「かなしみの土地」にこの地の悲劇が展開される種子が埋め込まれたように思われる。

「1　百年まえの蝶」では、ロシアやウクライナに向かう飛行機の窓の外の雲海に一羽の蝶が舞っているのを幻視する。

《ふと一羽の蝶が舞っていたと見たのは幻にちがいないが／こたびは別れて西ひがし、／振りかへりつゝ去りにけり。／一八九四年五月十六日未明の二十五歳の青年の思いと／一九九四年五月十六日そのことを思う者の思いと／に　架けるものはあるか》

若松氏は百年前の五月十六日に命を絶った北村透谷の詩「雙蝶のわかれ」を引用して、日本の近代・現代の詩や詩論的な評論の原点を創り出した詩人に思いを馳せている。透谷の詩や代表的な詩論的な評論である「内部生命論」などの志を引き継ぎたいという思いを新たにし、その透谷の志の力を借りたいと願ったのではないか。偶然にも百年前の五月十六日に他愛や平和主義や内面化の重要性を問うて他界した透谷に対して、百年後に放射性物質で汚染されて苦悩するウクライナのチェルノブイリの地を目撃するために旅立つ若松氏は、透谷の他界や苦悩するチェルノブイ

リである別世界に旅立つという意味で、何か共通する思いを抱いて窓の外に透谷の分身である一羽の蝶を想起したのではないか。

「2　五月のキエフに」では、キエフの五月の街並みを讃美して、ロシアの作曲家とウクライナの国民的な詩人を次のように書き記す。

《古い石造りの街のなかぞらを綿毛がさすらっている／ポプラの綿毛だ／白い花をつけたマロニエ並木は石造りの街なみに似つかわしい／キエフはヨーロッパでもっとも緑に富む都市だという／／五月のフレシャーチク通りを人びとは楽しんでいる》

若松氏はキエフの街路のポプラの綿毛や、マロニエ並木でゆったりと散歩する人びとがキエフの町を愛し寛いでいる光景を描写する。と同時に「起伏の多い道は住む人びとのこころの屈折を語っているか」とも語り、ウクライナの民衆の苦難の歴史を思いやっている。そして二人の芸術家の名前を挙げて、古都であり芸術の都であることを次のように記す。

《ムソルグスキイの「キエフの門」をたずね／ウクライナの人びとが誇る詩人の名まえを私は記憶した／マロニエはシェフチェンコに捧げる花か》

ロシアのムソルグスキイが作曲した「展覧会の絵」の「キエフの大門」は友への鎮魂の思いを気高く表現し、一度聴いたら忘れられない心に残る名曲だろう。それに因んだ「キエフの門」を若松氏は訪ねる。またタラス・シェフチェンコは、ロシア語でなくウクライナ語で初めて記された詩集『コブザール』によって国民的な詩人で、ロシア将校にもてあそばれた娘「カテルィーナ」の目を伏せた悲しみの表情が胸に迫ってくる絵画シリーズを描いた画家でもある。若松氏は「マロニエは

53

シェフチェンコに捧げる花か」と、ウクライナの人びとが十九世紀の詩人シェフチェンコの銅像を公園に作り、それを誇りに思っていることに深く感銘を受けたに違いない。

「3 風景を断ちきるもの」では、若松氏はウクライナ・ベラルーシ国境地帯の緊張感を目撃し、その国境地帯を語る時に、次の二つの映画の国境場面を想起している。映画は註によるとテオ・アンゲロプロス監督作品「こうのとり、たちずさんで」（一九九一年、ギリシャ）と、ヴィム・ヴェンダース監督作品「ベルリン・天使の詩」（一九八八年、西ドイツ・フランス）だ。福島・東北を基盤としている若松氏の詩作が、時に世界的な視野に転換されていくのは、学生時代から晩年に至るまで海外の映画を見続けていた影響によるものだったことが分かる。若松氏はウクライナとベラルーシとその先に続くロシアとの国境を目撃して、次のような詩行を生み出していったのだ。

《テオ・アンゲロプロスの映画の一シーンをまねて／ギリシャ・アルバニア・ユーゴスラヴィア国境地帯の／川や湖の多い映画のなかの風景と／ウクライナ・ベラルーシ国境地帯の／目前にひろがるドニエプル川支流の低地との／あまりの相似／けげんな表情で私を見る国境警備員／片脚立ちの姿は飛び立つことができょうか／こうのとり、たちずさんで／（略）／私たちが地図のうえにひいた境界は／私たちのこころにもつながっていて／私たちを差別する／私たちを難民にする／私たちが国境で足止めされているあいだに／牛乳缶を積んだ小型トラックが／ウクライナからベラルーシへと国境を越えていった／こともなげに／空中の放射性物質も／風にのって／幻蝶のように》

これらの詩行を読めば思い当たるように、若松氏は、二〇二二年二月二十四日にベラルーシか

54

ら国境を越えてウクライナを侵略したロシア軍が行った「私たちを差別する／私たちを難民にする／私たちを狙撃する」という光景を、一九九四年四月に予言のように透視していたとも感じられる。詩「6　神隠しされた街」が東電福島原発事故を予言した詩だと言われてきたが、私は今回のロシアのウクライナ侵略などを若松氏は予言のように、詩「3　国境を断ちきるもの」の中の三行で書き記していたと感じている。もし若松氏が生きていたら、人類の中に国境を越えて他国を蹂躙するという愚かな行為を反復してしまうことに対して、東電福島原発事故後と同様に、恐れていたことが再び現実化してしまい、激しい怒りをもって詩や評論を書き上げたに相違ないだろう。

「4　蘇生する悪霊」では、チェルノブイリ原子力発電所四号炉の石棺を間近に目撃した時の衝撃を語っている。ある意味で若松氏の予言に満ちた言葉は、次の「蘇生する悪霊」のような人類の呪われた「悪霊」が生み出してしまう最悪の結果を感受してしまう精神性を宿しているかも知れない。

《目前に／写真で見なれた／チェルノブイリ原子力発電所四号炉／《石棺》／悪しき形相で／まがまがしく／コンクリート五〇万㎥と／鉄材六〇〇〇tとで／封じた冥王プルートの悪霊／その悪霊が蘇生／しそうだという今にも／はげしく反応する線量計／悪霊の気／計測不能／「五分間だけ」／と案内人だが／アスファルト広場／石棺観光用展望台／ではなく焼香台／足もとに埋葬されている汚染物質／五分とここにいたくはない／痛くはないが／私たちは冒されている》

たぶん、若松氏の旅の目的はこの《石棺》を直視することだったが、それは生きた「悪霊」であり、線量計は振り切れて「計測不可能」で、「五分間だけ」と言われたが、すぐにも逃げ出したかったようだ。なぜなら「私たちは冒されている」と、放射性物質が押し寄せてくる言い知れぬ恐怖を肌で感じたからだろう。その意味で若松氏の恐怖感の旅の大きな目的は果たされたのであり、チェルノブイリ原発事故の八年後にこの「悪霊」の恐怖感を書き記し伝えたことがこの連作の優れた功績であったと思われる。またその「悪霊」は森林に降り注ぎ《ニンジン色の森》を出現させて、「人びとの不安の形象」となり、伐採されて埋葬されたという。しかし今回のロシア軍の将校はその「赤い森」を掘り起こし、塹壕を掘らせるように兵士たちに指示をした。その結果、ロシア兵たちは放射性物質に冒されていったことは間違いない。チェルノブイリ（チョルノービリ）の悲劇はロシア兵たちに伝えられてはいなかったことが明らかになった。

「5 《死》に身を曝す」では、事故後の「チェルノブイリ三〇kmゾーン」の日常を伝えている。

《チェルノブイリ三〇kmゾーン》の境界にゲートがある。ゲート脇から立入禁止区域を限る鉄線を張った粗末な柵が延々とつづいている。ここまでは緑うつくしい穀物畑が視野いっぱいに広がっていたが、柵の内側は荒れるにまかせた畑に赤枯れた草が所在なげに立ちつくしている。

私たちが迎えを待つあいだに、キエフ方面から三台のバスがやってきた。乗って来た人たちは別のバスに乗り換える。汚染されていないバスと汚染されているバスとゲートを境に別にしているのだろう。さまざまな年齢の彼ら彼女らはチェルノブイリ原子力発電所で働いている人たちである。発電所やその関連施設で二週間勤務しては交替するのだという。三〇

kmゾーンは立入禁止がたてまえだが、想像以上に多くの人たちが生活しているらしい。事故のあった四号炉に隣接する一～三号炉は稼働しているし、私たちが説明を受け、昼食をとった国際学術調査センターもゾーンの内側にある。ほかにも研究施設などがあるとのことだ。

バスで五、六号炉近くを通りかかったとき、人工池で釣りをしている人たちを見かけた。昼休みの気ばらしだというが、まさか釣った魚を食べることはあるまいと思うものの、おそらく汚染されているにちがいない人工池で平気で遊んでいる様子におどろいてしまった。四号炉の《展望台》では持参した線量計のカウンターが振り切れてしまい、私たちが浮き足立っているのに、すぐそばを作業員たちが日常的なこととして通り過ぎて行く。ゾーンのなかをバスに同乗して案内してくれたのは未婚の若い女性であった。将来の出産を考えれば働くべきところではないと思うのだが、そのことはわきまえていて勤務しているのだそうだ。

若松氏は、汚染され立入禁止の三〇kmゾーンの内と外でバスを乗り換えることによって、発電所や関連施設で働く人びとが二週間交替で働くことを知る。また破壊された四号炉の《石棺》近くで線量計がいまだ振り切れるような現状でも、昼休みに作業員たちが人工池で釣りをしたり、ゾーン内のバスガイドが未婚の女性であることに驚かされる。被曝の危険性への対応が不十分で、避難先に馴染めずにゾーン内の村々に戻った高齢者たち『死』に身を曝す」人びとの紹介の後には、この引用した部分の後には、この原発事故から八年後の世界を知って、若松氏は仮に東電福島第一原発が臨界事故を起こしたら、自分の暮らす南相馬市など三〇kmゾーンの市町村が一体どのような情況になるのか、想像もしたくなかったことだが、事

故後の世界が天啓のように想像され透視されたに違いない。若松氏は「5 《死》に身を曝す」において「発電所やその関連施設で二週間勤務」する人びとや以前住んでいた村々に帰還している高齢者たちを書き記すことによって、次の「6 神隠しされた街」のイメージが立ち上がってきたのだろう。

2

「6 神隠しされた街」が生まれてくるためには、黙示録の「ニガヨモギ」に触れたプロローグから始まり、1〜5までの経験を辿っていくことが必要だった。そして若松氏はチェルノブイリ（チョルノービリ）の経験を東電福島第一原発に次のように転換し、応用させていったのだろう。

《千百台のバスに乗って／プリピャチ市民が二時間のあいだにちりぢりに／近隣三村をあわせて四万九千人が消えた／四万九千人といえば／私の住む原町市の人口にひとしい／さらに／原子力発電所中心半径三〇kmゾーンは危険地帯とされ／十一日目の五月六日から三日のあいだに九万二千人が／あわせて約十五万人／人びとは一〇〇kmや一五〇km先の農村にちりぢりに消えた／半径三〇kmゾーンといえば／東京電力福島第一原子力発電所を中心に据えると／双葉町　大熊町　富岡町／楢葉町　浪江町　広野町／川内村　都路村　葛尾村／小高町　いわき市北部　そして私の住む原町市がふくまれる／こちらもあわせて約十五万人／私たちが消えるべき先はどこか／私たちはどこに姿を消せばいいのか／事故六年のちに避難命令が出た村さえもある／事故八年のちの旧プリピャチ市に／私たちは入った》

「私の住む原町市」は後に「小高町」と合併して「南相馬市」になった。若松氏はその「原町市」は「プリピャチ市民」の四万九千人とほぼ人口が同じであるという類似性に気づき、近未来にきっと同じことが起こるのではないかという恐怖感に襲われたに違いない。チェルノブイリ原発の三〇kmゾーンの人口は十五万人だが、東電福島第一原発の半径三〇kmゾーンも十五万人であった。

若松氏には、現場を「身体で感じ」て、さらに宇宙からの俯瞰的な地理感覚や人口統計的な数字の類似性から一挙に破壊されていく未来都市を予知し、そこに生きる人びとの在りようを透視してしまう、詩的想像力が存在していたのだろう。若松氏は「原発事故を予言した」と言われたが、自らは「予言」という言葉を好んではいなかった。その「予言」という言葉のことを、それを否定して、事実を突き詰めていくとそのように感じられたという意味のことを語っていたように思う。参考になるのは著作集第二巻『極端粘り族の系譜』第三章「インタビュー・対談」の〈南相馬伝説の詩人〉若松丈太郎インタビュー」で、著作集全三巻の装画写真を提供してくれたカメラマン・すぎた和人氏の質問に答えて次のように語っている。

《私も詩を書く時は頭の中で考える事よりも身体で感じる事を、それが見えないものであっても観る、聞こえない音であっても聴く、そしてそれを表現するのです》

若松氏の「予言」や「予知」に対する違和感やそれに代わる解答としての詩作することの「見えないものであっても観る」姿勢が、その肉声に宿っているように考えられる。

「7 囚われた人たち」では、被曝したキエフ小児科・産婦人科研究所の病院の子どもたちに会った際に感じたことを伝えている。

59

《キエフ小児科・産婦人科研究所の病院に入院している子どもたちに会って、ウクライナとベラルーシの子どもたちは囚われ人なのではあるまいかという思いをいだいた。医師と異国人とが通訳を介して自分たちを話題にしているその片言隻句のなかから、自分の貶められている不条理な状況についての情報を読みとろうと、子どもたちは注意力を集中している様子であった。子どもたちはおとなが思い込んでいるよりはるかに真実の核心にせまって正しい理解に達しているものである。私は子どもたちのそんな様子を見ながら、半世紀まえのフリョーラとグラーシャのことを思い出していた。ふたりは、一九四三年にドニエプル川の上流であるベラルーシの小さな村でおこなわれたナチスの犯罪を告発した映画「炎／628」のなかの少年と少女である。かつて私はこのフリョーラとグラーシャのことにふれて「冬に」という詩を書いた。》

若松氏は、子どもたちが日本人たちの質問によって、自分たちが置かれている身体の変容について「真実の核心にせまって正しい理解に達している」ことを知ったらしい。その子どもたちを見ながら同時に、若松氏はロシア・ベラルーシの映画でエレム・クリモフ監督「炎／628」を想起していた。ベラルーシの少年がロシア・ベラルーシの少年が村を守るために赤軍パルチザンに入るが、そこで少年が見たものはナチスドイツが628村とそこで暮らす人びとを犯して皆殺しにする光景だった。延々と続く虐殺場面に遭遇しその少年の顔は最後には老人のような顔になってしまうという映画だと言う。若松氏はキエフの小児科で治療を受けている子どもたちに、映画の主人公フリョーラの顔を重ねて、甲状腺癌などで苦悩しそれでも希望を心に抱く子どもたちの未来を深く憂慮していたの

かも知れない。

「8　苦い水の流れ」では、「プロローグ　ヨハネ黙示録」に出てきた「水の三分の一がニガヨモギのように苦くなった。／水が苦くなったため多くの人びとが死んだ。」という予言の言葉が本当に二十世紀に起こってしまったことが記されている。

《広大なドニエプル川の流域／ウクライナだけではなく／ロシアやベラルーシもその水源にして／プリピャチ川が合流するあたりに／チェルノブイリがある／上流から三分の一のあたり／セシウム一三七による汚染地図をひろげると／上流三分の一地域が彩色されていて／苦い水を川におし流している／チェルノブイリ一〇㎞ゾーン内の／ニガヨモギが茂る土饅頭の下に／八百の土饅頭の下に汚染物質が葬られている／八百の土饅頭が地下水を苦い水にかえている／《石棺》がひびわれはじめたと／熱と重みによって地盤の状態は危機的だと／発電所の人工池から水はプリピャチ川に流れ／プリピャチ川はドニエプル川に流れ／ゆたかなドニエプル川は苦い水を内蔵して流れゆく》

この「8　苦い水の流れ」において、原発事故が河川や地下水などを汚染し続け、途方もない十万年もの間続くことの恐ろしさを再認識させる。若松氏はチェルノブイリ近くの二つの川の合流地点付近を目撃し、汚染され伐採された木々の埋められた「八百の土饅頭」から流れ出す「汚染物質」を幻視していたに違いない。若松氏のこの「苦い水」への想像力こそは、仮に福島で原発事故が起きた十七年後に、山河の森や河川で何が起こるかを暗示していたことは間違いないだろう。

「9　白夜にねむる水惑星」では、モスクワ経由で帰国する際に見た白夜の光に若松氏の祈りが

込められている。

《モスクワ午後八時離陸の旅客機は／太陽を左手に定め／時を停め／浮遊しているかのようだ／ここは白夜で／夕陽はそのまま朝の光を放ちはじめる／よどんだ夜の地表を／川は流れつづけているだろう／一日のはじまりをまえに／人びとは不安なつかのまのねむりに沈んでいるだろう／夢のなか蝶は舞っているだろうか／窓外に蝶はいない》

若松氏は深夜のシベリア上空で白夜を見たのかも知れない。その時間にチェルノブイリ、キエフ、ウクライナ・ベラルーシ国境やそこで出会った人びとを想起したのだろう。ドニエプル川とプリピャチ川の「苦い水」と共に生きるウクライナの人びとに、北村透谷の「内部生命」を宿した蝶が生き続けることを願ったのかも知れない。

最後の「エピローグ　かなしみのかたち　東京国立博物館で国宝法隆寺展をみる」では、若松氏はウクライナの子どもたちへの思いを次のように語り、連作を終えている。

《日光菩薩像をまえ／に　ウクライナの子どもたちを思った／いまさらのように気づいた／ひとのかなしみは千年まえ／も　いまも変わりないのだ／そして過去にあった／ものは　将来にも予定されてあるのだ／あふれるなみだ／あふれるドニエプルの川づら／あふれる苦い水》

日光菩薩像は、一千もの光明を発して、世界を照らし出し、様々な苦しみの底にある無明の闇を滅ぼしてくれると言われている。若松氏の葬儀は、本人の遺志を尊重し無宗教で行われた。生前からも自分が無宗教であることを公言し、その影響を祖父からのものであることも記していた。しかしながら若松氏のこの「かなしみの土地」のエピローグなどを読むと、様々な宗派や教団に

は与しないが、不幸な人びとの苦しみを癒そうとして彫られた仏像を生み出した、救済としての宗教心を深く理解していて、豊かにそのような精神を宿していることが読み取れ、ウクライナの子どもたちを慈しむ精神性を強く感じる。この精神性は出身地の岩手県の詩人で子どもの幸せを願って詩や童話を書いた宮沢賢治とも共通するものがあると私は感じている。若松氏は長年にわたり高校の国語教師を続け、いつも図書館担当になり良書を薦める傍ら、「教師や親に相談できない本当に困ったことがあったら、丈太郎先生のところへ行け」と、子どもたちの間で言われていたと関係者たちから聞いている。このような未来に生きる子どもたちの幸せを願ってこの「かなしみの土地」十一篇が書かれたに違いない。その意味で若松氏にとって本当の予言や予知的な言葉とは、きっと子どもたちの真の慈しみに満ちた熟慮の言葉であると物語っているようだ。読解を深めるためにたちを解き放つための、大人たちの真の慈しみに満ちた熟慮の言葉であると物語っているようだ。読解を深めるために

「かなしみの土地」十一篇は、まだ読まれ始めたばかりのような気がする。読解を深めるために著作集第三巻『評論・エッセイ』の冒頭の『イメージのなかの都市　非詩集成1』の「キエフ・モスクワ　一九九四年五月十八日　キエフ」、詩「いくつもの川があって」や詩「夜の惑星　三篇」なども参考になるだろう。

『若松丈太郎著作集　全三巻』を通読することは大変な労力だが、例えばこの「かなしみの土地」十一篇からでも読まれることをお勧めしたい。この代表詩篇を理解できれば他の詩篇や評論・エッセイもより理解度が増すだろう。

Ⅱ章　若松丈太郎の代表詩篇十五篇

夜の森 一

森はおまえの恥毛
地平低く愛に澱む
その枝を重ね合う木々
夜の森
けものたちは潜み
けものたちは木の間の星を眺め
けものたちは匂いをかぎあう
雨が近いのだろうか
絶え間ない星の明滅
突風
枝々がたわみ
木々がたわみ
森がたわみ

夜がたわみ
愛する女よ
ぼくらも　けものたちに倣い
森の洞に夜をすごし　星にぼくらを写し
ふたりのからだの匂いをかぎ合おう
いつでもぼくらの望むものはもうひとつの別のものだった
いつでもぼくらはもうひとつの別のものに裏切られた
ぼくらは神話を恐れ果てなくもうひとつの別のものを望んだ
もうひとつの別のものとはぼくらにとって何なのか
おまえの匂いを焚き
ぼくの匂いを焚き
ぼくらの匂いは森にひろがり
ぼくらは星をひろう

網膜を横切った白い速度は何なのか
ぼくの魂か肉体か
おまえのそれか
死者のそれか

67

あれがぼくらの望んだ**もうひとつの別のもの**だろうか

森がたわみ

夜がたわみ

愛がたわみ

愛する女よ

せめて　ぼくらも　けものたちに倣い

ぼくらの匂いを焚こう

雨期が来る

地平に低い夜の森に

突風

夜の森　四

一九五七年　アメリカの原爆実験シリーズ第十六回実験のとき、
同時に「神経テスト」が行われた。

時間の経過をアナウンスする監視所

は　非情の黒さで立つ

一九五七年九月二日　ネバダ

わたしの名は　ジョー

であっても　トミー

であっても　かまわない

栄誉ある第八二空挺師団

に　われわれが属し

ストーベル大尉の指揮下にあること　われわれには

それのほかはない

神の思召しであろう

周辺の森
は　黒く潜み
けものたちのいきづき
に　低くゆれる
午前五時
は　とうに過ぎた

けれど
けれど
朝に近づくことは
朝から遠ざかることだ
神に近づくことは
神から遠ざかることではなかろうか

白いけものが飛んだ
あれはなに

どこから　どこへ
同様に　神の思召し
なのか

〈暗いなあ　ずいぶん〉

爆発点
からの　四四〇〇メートル
は安らぎの　あるいは　慰めの
距離
で　はたして　ありうるか
遠い山々へ
白いけものを飛ばせたものは
本能
ああ　われわれは　本能も捨てよう

この夜明け
森は夜

に　退く

〈暗いねえ　きみの瞳のように〉

一切が　われわれの前に
存在しないのではなかろうか
塹壕も
コンクリート壁も
鋼鉄製掩蓋も
そして
神も
われわれの周辺には
存在しないのだ

鳥たちも飛ばない
雲がひき裂かれ
星のまばたきは　わたしの思惟のように　低く　さまよい　ぼろぼろだ
けものたちも歩かない

〈暗くはないよ
　明るいいじゃないか
　明るいと言うんだよ
　こんなときには〉

絞首台に立つ者は　その階段を　数えながらのぼることだろう

〈一〇秒前⋯⋯〉
一三⋯⋯一二⋯⋯一一⋯⋯

舌で唇を湿す
喉を鳴らす
だれかが　つぶやく
〈死刑宣告〉
わななき声で
あるいは　わなないているのは　わたし
の耳なのか
それとも　世界の唇や耳なのか
夜の森

73

に　確かなものはない

時間経過のアナウンスは　われわれの

判事

教誨師

死刑執行人

時すらも確かでない

生も死も

死刑　違う

自殺　違う

決闘

背を向け合い　歩む

生と死

の間を　低くさまよう　わたしの

思惟

そして

そして

わたしの決闘の相手は……

遠いコヨーテの声も　空にすわれ　いまは聞こえない

からだをまるめ
頭を膝につける
無力なダンゴムシの防御
手に力が入り　握った砂が　こぼれ落ちる

わたしの名は　ジョー
であっても　トミー
であっても　かまわない
一匹の虫けら
に過ぎないのならば

ない
われわれの周辺には

ない
いっさいがわれわれの前に
ない

無

父はよく言った
〈無は有を生ず〉と
どこで
こころでか
わたしの
わたしのこころ
に生じ　おののいているもの
は　なに
恐怖か
懇願か
反逆か

……二……一

○ わたしは

望郷小詩──宮沢賢治による variations

水沢

向ふの雲まで野原のやうだ／あすこらへんが水沢か／君のところはどの辺だらう

（「五輪峠」──『春と修羅』第二集）

あすこらへんが水沢かと
焼石岳（やけいしだけ）の尾根みちで
茫々々の北上平野をふりかえる
種山高原（たねやま）や五輪峠（ごりん）はそのむこう
こちらむきで賢治が目にした眺望を
こちらがわからぼくらはながめる
君のところはどの辺だろう
日高見（ひたかみ）のくにばら
畑をひらき
田に水をいれ

78

野に馬をはなち

林間にけものを追った

まつろわぬ部族集団の楽土

あすこらへんが水沢なら

あれが衣川（ころもがわ）

あすこが平泉

水陸万頃（ばんけい）　豊饒のくにばら

集落は島々となってうかぶ

むこうの雲まで多島海のようだ

日高見のくにから野焼きのけむりがあがる

千五百年後のぼくらにむけて発信するのろし

人首町（ひとかべまち）

雪や雑木にあさひがふり／丘のはざまのいっぽん町は／あさましいまで光ってゐる

（『人首町』―『春と修羅』第二集）

丘のはざまのいっぽん町がつきるところ

鳴瀬川の吊り橋にゆく角から二軒目

酒屋の本棚に『野球界』のバックナンバーがあった

丘のはざまのいっぽん町のクラブチームが鳴瀬倶楽部

叔父もメンバーだった鳴瀬倶楽部

十五キロ川下のぼくらの町にきてゲームをした

ビー玉やぜんまいの綿毛を芯に毛糸をまいたボールであそんでいたぼくらは彼らのプレーにあ

こがれた

ずいぶんけわしい山道を木炭バスはあえぎ登ったように記憶しているが

いま人首町への道にはふしぎに急坂がない

酒屋のうらは鳴瀬川

いわなやはやが瀬にうろこを光らせていて

いろりにならんだ焼き串が香ばしかった

酒屋は母がそだった家

ぼくがうまれた家でもある

丘のはざまのいっぽん町には伝説がのこされている

蝦夷（えみし）の酋長悪路王（あくろおう）の一族に十五、六歳の少年がいたという

少年は征夷軍からのがれ大森山の岩窟にかくれたという

首討たれた人首丸はうつくしかったという

ぼくは悪路王の末裔であろうか
そうではなくとも人首丸をかくまった村人の子孫か
丘のはざまのいっぽん町の街道脇に流れのはやい水路があって
うけそこなったボールを追って足をふみはずしたことがある
ながされながら水面に顔が浮いたとき
征夷軍の射た矢がかすめ飛んだ

北上川

北上川は熒気（けいき）をながしィ／山はまひるの思睡を翳す
（北上川は熒気をながしィ）——『春と修羅』第二集

千年むかしの光をうかべ北上川は流れる
この橋をわたり八キロ離れた高等学校へ通学したことがある
桜木橋に自転車をとめ川風をうける
岸の木だちが川風にそよぐ
風のように過ぎるものがある
あいつか

橋上に立つとここは全宇宙の中心のように思えるのだ

遠く小さく岩手山も早池峰山も見える

東に種山・姥石高原

西に焼石岳・駒ケ岳

やや上流の段丘上が胆沢城趾

やや下流が跡呂井

蝦夷の酋長アテルイの根拠地と伝えられる

はるばるの贄となったアテルイ

討たれた首は都の辻で夕焼け空を睥睨した

風のように過ぎるものがある

あいつか

あいつとは誰だ

橋上に立つといまは全時間の中心のように思えるのだ

千年むかしの光をうかべ北上川は流れる

死んでしまったおれに

ジョー・オダネル撮影 「焼き場にて、長崎*」のために

おれだ
おれが写っている

と

写真を眼にした瞬間
国民学校初等科四年のおれだ

と

正面前方に視線を据えている
一文字に口を結んでいる
丸刈りの頭
指をぴしっとそろえ
その中指は半ズボンの両脇の縫い目に沿わせている
はだしの踵をそろえ
つま先びらきに立っている

おれたちがからだにたたき込まれた姿勢
〈気を付け〉の姿勢
にはちがいないが
少年は上体をやや前傾させている
腰をわずかに折って

これは〈礼〉の姿勢だ
〈礼〉の姿勢の背中に弟
少年は弟を背負っている
背負い帯でしっかりと背負っている
弟は首をのけぞらせている
弟は兄の背中ですでに息絶えている

死んだ弟を背負った少年のまなざしを見たか
かなしみに耐えている少年のまなざしを見たか
かなしみに耐えつつ視線は前方に据えられている
かなしみに耐えつつ視線はなにに向けられているのか
なにに対しての〈礼〉なのか

地上に死があふれ
生と死とが入りまじり
生と死とが背中あわせで
兄と弟とが一枚の布をさかいに
生と死とに別れ
兄と弟の生と死とが入れかわっても
死神はみずからのまちがいに気づくはずもなく

地上に死者があふれ
折り重ね積みあげられ
死者は荼毘のほのおに包まれる
ほのおが少年の頬をほてらす
父や母であり兄弟であり友人であるかもしれないおびただしい死者たちへの
少年自身であるかもしれないおびただしい死者たちへの
〈礼〉は別れの挨拶である
かろうじて死をまぬがれた者からの挨拶である

少年は背負い帯をほどき

弟を背中からおろし
やがて
ほのおをあげて燃える弟を
少年自身であるかもしれない死者を
かなしみに耐えつつ記憶する

おれだ
十歳のおれが写っている
と
写真のなかの死者であるおれに対し
かろうじて生き残った者からの挨拶を返す
挨拶を返しつつ
半世紀を経たいまも
世紀を新しくするいまも
あの少年のかなしみが存在する地上の現実を

＊ジョー・オダネル写真集『トランクの中の日本』（一九九五年・小学館）九七ページ所収。一九四五年、戦後の長崎。
川岸に設けられた遺体焼き場にやって来た、背中に死んだ幼い弟を背負った十歳ほどの少年を撮影した写真。

霧の向こうがわとこちらがわ

1　ジェラゾヴァ・ヴォーラの空

日陰のベンチを選んで待つ

マロニエ

ニセアカシア

野いばら

花ばなのあいだをたわむれてきた風

頬にここちよく

五月のヨーロッパをポプラの綿毛が飛んでいる

ウクライナ平原の空からも

クラコフやプラハのほうへ

ベオグラードやサライェヴォのほうへ

ちいさな種子をはこんで

夏の雪が飛んでいる
白壁に蔦がはうショパンの生家の庭にも
ささやかな演奏会場である庭にも

ピアニストはアレクサンダー・ガヴリリュク
ショパンが祖国を離れた年ごろの青年
隣国ウクライナ嘱望の俊才だ
最初の演奏曲は「幻想曲　ヘ短調」作品49
その主旋律を中田喜直は「雪の降る町を」に借用したようだ
五月の空は青く
ワルシャワ郊外ジェラゾヴァ・ヴォーラ村を
雪ならぬポプラの綿毛が飛んでいる

演奏にあわせるかのよう
空の高みから雲雀の声
ブラウニングなら 〈The lark's on the wing.〉*
上田敏なら 〈揚雲雀なのりいで、〉
そして

〈God's in his heaven……
All's right with the world!〉

と結ぶのだが
ほんとうに今ここは 〈事もなし〉 なのだが

ヨーロッパのここかしこから
さまざまな人びとが思いおもいに
東洋の韓国や日本からも集い
それぞれの思いをいだいて
「バラード」に耳を傾けている
「スケルツォ」を愉しんでいる
犬を散歩させる人が庭先をよぎって行く
日常を離れた非日常にいて
非日常に日常がまぎれこんで
日常の厚みのようなものを見せて
「ポーランド風舞曲」をBGMに見立てるかのよう
自転車の少女が庭先を通りすぎて行く

ほんとうに今ここは〈事もなし〉なのだが
この瞬間この場所だけのことかもしれない
幻景を見ているにすぎないのかもしれない
演奏されているピアノ曲も幻聴で
花ばなのあいだをたわむれてきた風と
五月の青い空を飛んできたポプラの綿毛と
たしかなのはこうしたものだけかもしれない

＊R・ブラウニング「ピパの唄」。上田敏『海潮音』では「春の朝」と訳されている。

90

みなみ風吹く日

1

岸づたいに吹く
南からの風がこちよい
沖あいに波を待つサーファーたちの頭が見えかくれしている
チェルノブイリ事故直後に住民十三万五千人が緊急避難したエリアの内側
福島第一原子力発電所から北へ二十五キロ
福島県原町市北泉(きたいずみ)海岸

福島第一原子力発電所から北へ八キロ
福島県双葉郡浪江町南棚塩(みなみたなしお)
福島県双葉郡浪江町南棚塩

たとえば
一九七八年六月
福島第一原子力発電所から北へ八キロ
福島県双葉郡浪江町南棚塩
舛倉隆(ますくらたかし)さん宅の庭に咲くムラサキツユクサの花びらにピンク色の斑点があらわれた
けれど
原発操業との有意性は認められないとされた

91

たとえば

一九八〇年一月報告
福島第一原子力発電所一号炉南放水口から八百メートル
海岸土砂　ホッキ貝　オカメブンブクからコバルト60を検出

たとえば

一九八〇年六月採取
福島第一原子力発電所から北へ八キロ
福島県双葉郡浪江町幾世橋
小学校校庭の空気中からコバルト60を検出

たとえば

一九八八年九月
福島第一原子力発電所から北へ二十五キロ
福島県原町市栄町
わたしの頭髪や体毛がいっきに抜け落ちた
いちどの洗髪でごはん茶碗ひとつ分もの頭髪が抜け落ちた

むろん

原発操業との有意性が認められることはないだろう

ないだろうがしかし

南からの風がこちよい

波間にただようサーファーたちのはるか沖

二艘のフェリーが左右からゆっくり近づき遠ざかる

気の遠くなる時間が視える

世界の音は絶え

すべて世はこともなし

あるいは

来るべきものをわれわれは視ているか

2

一九七八年十一月二日

チェルノブイリ事故の八年まえ

福島第一原子力発電所三号炉

圧力容器の水圧試験中に制御棒五本脱落

日本最初の臨界状態が七時間三十分もつづく
東京電力は二十九年を経た二〇〇七年三月に事故の隠蔽をようやく認める

あるいは
一九八四年十月二十一日
福島第一原子力発電所二号炉
原子炉の圧力負荷試験中に臨界状態のため緊急停止
東京電力は二十三年を経た二〇〇七年三月に事故の隠蔽をようやく認める

制御棒脱落事故はほかにも
一九七九年二月十二日　福島第一原子力発電所五号炉
一九八〇年九月十日　福島第一原子力発電所二号炉
一九九三年六月十五日　福島第二原子力発電所三号炉
一九九八年二月二十二日　福島第一原子力発電所四号炉
などなど二〇〇七年三月まで隠蔽ののち

福島第一原子力発電所から南南西へはるか二百キロ余
東京都千代田区大手町
経団連ビル内の電気事業連合会ではじめてあかす

二〇〇七年十一月
福島第一原子力発電所から北へ二十五キロ
福島県南相馬市北泉海岸
サーファーの姿もフェリーの影もない
世界の音は絶え
南からの風が肌にまとう
われわれが視ているものはなにか

町がメルトダウンしてしまった

1

米屋　八百屋　魚屋　豆腐屋　味噌醤油屋　漬物屋

羊羹屋　煎餅屋　菓子屋　駄菓子屋

酒屋　油屋　牛乳屋　氷屋　荒物屋　炭屋　亜炭屋

呉服屋　洋品店　仕立屋　織屋　網屋　染物屋　洗濯屋

文房具屋　本屋　時計屋　写真屋　印刷屋　新聞屋

薬屋　医院　産婆　床屋　髪結い　下駄屋　靴屋

花屋　造花屋　箔屋　飾屋　仏具屋　寺　教会

旅館　料理屋　食堂　芝居小屋　釣具屋

郵便局　銀行　信用金庫　質屋

バス会社　運送屋　馬車屋　博労　便利屋

材木屋　木工所　簞笥屋　建具屋　畳屋　布団屋　棟梁

瓦屋　トタン屋　ブリキ屋　金物屋　鋳物屋

鍋釜屋　鋳掛け屋　農具屋　蹄鉄屋

2

わたしが育った町は人口ほぼ一万人
端から端まで十五分も歩けば尽きる町並に
ぎっしりとさまざまな店が軒を並べていた
さまざまな職人が店先で仕事をしていた
暮らしてゆくためのたいがいのものは町のなかにあって
暮らしを支えあっている関係がうまく成立していたのだろう
障害のある人にも仕事があって
閉鎖的なムラではなく外にも開かれていて
ヨーロッパの〈シティ〉で市民文化が発祥したように
江戸時代末期ごろから昭和のはじめごろまでに
日本でも地方の小都市に市民文化が醸成されつつあった

そんな町の仕組みを壊したのが一億総動員体制だ
国民皆兵やら〈隣組〉やら愛国婦人会やらが
わたしが育った町を壊していった

3

福島県相馬郡小高町は小ぶりながら
わたしが育った町によく似た町だった
旧街道の一本道の中央に水路があって
暮らしを支えあっている町の人びととの関係を象徴していた
駒村・大曲省三の近所に五歳年長の余生・鈴木良雄と一歳年少の布鼓・原隆明がいた
彼らは俳句グループ渋茶会をつくって研鑽しあった
早世した良雄の『余生遺稿』を省三は自費で出版した
省三が『川柳辞彙』編纂に没頭して生活に困窮すると
隆明が省三の生活をさまざまなかたちで援助した
省三が亡くなると良雄の子安蔵は「駒村さんのことども」を書いて追悼した
隆明は自家の墓所に省三の墓を建ててその死を慰めた
平田良衛と二歳年少の鈴木安蔵とはともに相馬中学校と第二高等学校で学び
たがいに敬意をいだいて励ましあった
良衛はレーニン『何をなすべきか』を訳し『日本資本主義発達史講座』を編集した
安蔵は『憲法の歴史的研究』を著し『憲法草案要綱』を公表した

市民文化を醸成していた地方の小都市の仕組みを壊したのが一億総動員体制だ

98

国民皆兵やら〈隣組〉やら愛国婦人会やらが
大曲駒村や鈴木安蔵をはぐくんだ町を壊していった

4

暮らしを支えあう関係がなんとか残っていた地方の小都市に
アメリカ渡来の大型店が闖入してきた
まわりの小さな店がひとつまたひとつと店じまいした
豆腐屋が豆腐をつくるのをやめ
八百屋が店を閉め
仕立屋から職人がいなくなった
町なかにシャッターが降りたままの店がふえた

郊外により大きなスーパーマーケットが開業すると
町なかの大型店はさっさと撤退した
町なかを歩いている人がいなくなって
通りは車が移動するためだけのものになって
町は町としての機能をなくしてしまった

5

アメリカ渡来の核発電所が暴発して
核発電所から一五キロの小高町は《警戒区域》になった
《警戒区域》とは警戒していればいいのかというと
そうではなくて区域外に避難せよという指示だ
そこから出て行けという指示だ
核発電所のメルトダウンがあって
地方のどこにでもあるような町がメルトダウンしてしまった
いくつもの町がだれも住めない場所になってしまった
町は町でなくなってしまった

不条理な死が絶えない

戦争のない国なのに町や村が壊滅してしまった
あるいは天災だったら諦めもつこうが
いや天災だって諦めようがないのに
核災は人びとの生きがいを奪い未来を奪った

二〇一一年四月十二日、福島県相馬郡飯舘村
村が計画的避難区域に指定された翌朝
百二歳の村最高齢男性が服装を整えて自死した
「生きすぎた　おれはここから出たくない」

二〇一一年六月十一日、福島県相馬市玉野
出荷停止された原乳を捨てる苦しみの日々があって
四十頭を飼育していた五十四歳男性が堆肥舎で死亡

「原発で手足ちぎられ酪農家」

二〇一一年六月二十二日、福島県南相馬市原町区
家族と別れ自宅でのひとり暮らしもしたりして
九十三歳の女性が遺書四通を残して庭で自死した
「さようなら　私はお墓にひなんします」

二〇一一年七月一日、福島県伊達郡川俣町山木屋
計画的避難区域内の家に一時帰宅していてのこと
失職中の五十八歳女性が近くの空き地で焼身した
「避難したくない　元の暮らしをしたい」

二〇一二年五月二十八日、福島県双葉郡浪江町
商店を営んでいた町が警戒区域となって一年二ヵ月
六十二歳の男性が一時帰宅中に倉庫内で自死した
「もうこのまま戻れないんじゃないか」

遺族たちが東京電力を提訴・告訴しても

因果関係を立証できないと却下されるだろう

生きがいを奪われた人びとの死が絶えない

戦争のない国なのに不条理な死が絶えない

夷俘の叛逆

中華という思想があった
自らを世界の中央に君臨するものとし
四周を未開の地としてその住民を蔑視して
東夷・西戎・南蛮・北狄と呼んだ

中華思想は東海の島嶼に及んだ
ヤマト王権は東方や北方の先住民たちを
夷狄・蝦夷・蝦賊と名付けて従属させようとし
順化の程度によって夷俘・俘囚などと差別した

当然のこととしてレジスタンス活動が続発した
たとえば七七〇年代（宝亀年代）
七七〇（宝亀元）年、蝦夷反乱、賊地に逃げ還る

七七四（宝亀五）年、蝦夷反乱し桃生城に侵入する

七七六（宝亀七）年、志波・胆沢の蝦夷が叛逆する

七七七（宝亀八）年、蝦賊叛逆、出羽軍が敗れる

数日後には多賀城に侵入した

按察使の紀広純らを撃退し

七八〇（宝亀十一）年に伊治城で乱を起こし

夷俘を祖とする大領（郡司）伊治公呰麻呂がいた

奈良末期の陸奥国伊治郡に

呰麻呂の名は魁偉な容貌を連想させる

七八九（延暦八）年に大墓公阿弖流為が

胆沢の巣伏の戦いで

侵攻したヤマト王権の蝦夷征討軍を斥けたのは

宝亀の乱の九年のちのことである

呰麻呂や阿弖流為のように史書に記名されることなく

記憶の彼方に消えた蝦賊は数知れない

土人からヤマトへもの申す

米軍基地建設に抗議するウチナンチューに
ヤマトから派遣された警官のひとりが
「土人！」と罵声をあびせた

ウチナンチューが土人だば
おらだも土人でがす
そでがす　おら土着のニンゲンでがす
生まれてこのかた白河以南さ住んだことぁねぇ
〈東北の土人〉〈地人の夷狄〉でがす

電力業界内で言われてきたことば
「東電さんには〈植民地〉があって羨ましい」
東京電力は核発電所すべてを〈植民地〉に設置した

あげくに核災を起こして
地人のいのちと暮らしを奪った

福島から避難したこどもたちを
〈菌〉と呼ぶいじめが各地であったという

いじめを受けた子に一言
いじめっ子に言い返してやんなさい
「菌が嫌いならパンも納豆も食べてないだろうな」
「放射能が感染るってんだったら親に頼めよ
浜岡や東海の原発が福島原発よりも近くて怖い
再稼働に反対してくれ」
とでもね

一九五一年の日米安全保障条約によって
沖縄を米軍政下に二十年もゆだねて基地を集中させ
本土復帰後も占領者意識そのままの米軍関係者を
免法特権や治外法権で保障しつづけてる

〈わが国〉は主権の行使を怠ってる
植民地そのままの現状を容認しつづけてる
地人のいのちと暮らしを奪ってる

〈植民地の土人〉を迫害するヤマトよ
〈わが国〉と称する国土すべても植民地じゃないか
二重の植民地で暮らす怒りは限界を超えた
全米軍基地を撤去せよ
全核発電所を廃炉にしろ

こころのゆたかさ

大胆な造形力がある
こころに響くものがある
どうしてなんだろう
数千年以上も過去につくられたものに

ゆたかな生活感が伝わってくる
肌合いの実在感がある
どうしてなんだろう
数千年以上も地中に埋もれていたものに

自分の思いが込められているかと感じる
つよい親近感をおぼえる
どうしてなんだろう

数千年以上もつながりが失われていたものに

わたしたちの時代ってなんだろう
なにをしてきたのだろう
どんな時間を過ごしてきたのだろう

わたしたちの時代ってなんだろう
あるいはヒロシマ被爆以後なんだろう
あるいはソヴィエト連邦崩壊以後なのか
あるいは逆にもっと長い時間を考えるべきか

ルネサンスや大航海の時代ののち
宗教改革や市民改革あるいは産業革命ののち
五百年とか二百五十年とかのあいだ
わたしたちはなにをしてきたのだろう

わたしたちの時代ってなんだろう

ブッダが誕生したころから
孔子が死歿したころから
ペリクレスが民主政治を唱えたころから

わたしたちの時代とは
二千五百年ほどまえからを言うべきなのか
それ以前までさかのぼることは無理だとして

改革とか革命とかを
くりかえしたということは
そのたびに反動があったということだろう
わたしたちはどうしようもない生きものなのか

この百年あまりのあいだ
戦争がエポックメークになった
どうひいき目に見てもわたしたちは
どうしようもない生きものにちがいない

わたしたちは核爆弾をつかった
わたしたちは核発電をつかっている
わたしたちは国ぐるみの殺しあいをしてきた

わたしたちのあとの時代があるとして
あとの時代に遺すことを誇れるものを
わたしたちは創造しているのだろうか
さむざむしいものをしか遺せないのではないか

ペリクレスが生きた古代ギリシア
そのおなじころまでのこの島々には
一万年あまりものながいあいだを
縄文びとたちが暮らしていた
縄文びとたちが暮らしていた

生活環境に恵まれていたとは言えなかろうが
ゆたかな生きかたをしていたとは想像できる

火焔土器のオリジナリティに圧倒されるも
ひとのぬくもりを感じて共感してしまう
どこから獲得したのか
こころのなかからにちがいない

人面付土器　人形付土器　遮光器土偶
後ろ手を組んだ土偶　笑い顔の土偶
身ごもった土偶　こどもを抱いた土偶
こどもの手形や足形　土面

こころのゆたかさが見える
こんな魅力にとむものがほかにあろうか

三千年未来へのメッセージ

ササタケの編み籠にぎっしりと入れられ
三千年まえに貯蔵されていたという
南相馬市鹿島の鷺内遺蹟（さぎうち）から出土した
二百つぶを超える縄文晩期のオニグルミ

出土地に隣接する鷺内稲荷の案内板には
「暖冬清水の地」と書かれている
真野川と上真野川との氾濫原による
ゆたかな自然環境に恵まれて
クリやトチやクルミの木などが
たくさん自生していたことだろう
定住をはじめた人びとのメッセージを
清らかな地下水が三千年後に届けたのだ

こどものころに暮らしたわたしの町は
べつの町ではあるけれど
祖父母の家の裏の川岸にクルミの木
畑のある山にはクリの木
実を拾う楽しみがあった
縄文びととの暮らしをしのぶ

縄文びととは津波が及ばない場所を知っていた
鷺内も小高の浦尻貝塚もそうだ
浦尻貝塚は縄文期をとおして営まれた
アサリ　シジミ　カモ　シカ　イノシシ
スズキ　ハゼ　イワシ　タイ　ウナギ　フナ
恵まれたぜいたくな食卓だ

万葉時代になると大和びとが統治し
真野と名づけ真野の草原は歌枕とされた
四十年まえの地図によると

鷺内周辺に水田と桑畑の記号がたくさんあって
ゆたかな農村をイメージできる
けれど今は桑畑はもちろん水田もほとんどない
核災を被って住み処と暮らしを奪われ
やむなく避難しているひとびとの住宅地になった
多くの人は故郷への帰還をあきらめている

三千年後のひとびとにわたしたちは
どんなメッセージを届けることになるのだろう

軍備はいらない

わたしが生まれた年を起点にしてみる

七十年を遡ると一八六五年慶応元年

遠いと意識していた幕末が意外な近さにあった

八十年を遡ると一八五五年安政三年

欧米諸国が艦隊をさしむけ開国をせまっていた

このとき日本には戦争ができる軍備はなかった

そのことが幸いだったと思えてならない

その後の日本は軍拡の道をひたすら突き進んだ

一八七四年明治七年台湾出兵を嚆矢として

七十年のあいだ戦争をし続けてきた

相手国の多くのひとびとがその犠牲になった

日本の多くのひとびともその犠牲になった

国家という機構がひとをものとして扱った
わたしが生きた時代はいのちの尊厳を否認した
わたしが生まれて二年のちの一九三七年
ドイツの爆撃機がスペインのゲルニカを空爆した
日本軍が中国の南京で一般住民までも殺害した

無差別大量殺戮の時代がはじまった
銃器は単発銃から機関銃がつくりだされた
弾丸は大口径の砲弾や大型爆弾も使われた
火炎放射器や焼夷弾や毒ガスがひとのいのちを奪った
核爆発さえも大殺戮と大破壊の手段に換えた
国家という機構がひとさえも武器にした
人間爆弾　人間魚雷　特攻機　玉砕

一九四五年から七十年が過ぎたいまも
国家とか思想とか宗教とか
ひとがつくりだしたものが

ひとをさまざまな口実で区分けし差別している
ひとをものとして扱って道具にしている

第一次世界大戦から百年のあいだ
ひとがしてきたことの愚かさを思えば
戦争をしなかった日本の七十年は誇っていい
戦争ができる軍備を持たなかった幸いだった
けれど七十年という時間は記憶を失わせる
戦争ができる軍備を持つ愚かさを忘れさせる

ひとにはことばがある

住むところに困ることなく
家族となごやかに暮らし
となり近所のひとびとと会えば挨拶を交わす

食べものに困ることなく
身につけるものに困ることなく
行きたいところに行けて
したいことをして
言いたいことを言える

こうしたことに不自由がなければ
ひとはこころ穏やかでいられるはずだが

わたしたちは知っている
いま砲弾の破片で全身傷だらけの少女がいる
いま小銃を手にしている少年がいる
喫水線を遙かに超えて難民たちを乗せた小船に
なお乗り込もうとしているひとたちがいる
絶えることなく争いがつづいていて
いま不条理を被っているひとたちがいて
いま不条理な死を被っているひとたちがいる
そのことをわたしたちは知っている

十歳の夏まで戦争の時代を生きた体験から
わたしは願う
子や孫たちが不条理を被らないことを
すべてのひとびとが不条理を被らないことを
ひとはことばをもちいることができる
武力による争いを捨ててことばで解決しよう
すべてのひとびとが不条理を被らないよう

すべてのひとびとがこころ穏やかでいられるよう

いま不条理を被っているひとたちがいるかぎり
わたしたちはこころ穏やかではいられない

未知の若い友人へ

——市立中央図書館へのいざない

ひとはうまれるまえ
臍帯（さいたい）で母親の血とつながって
はじめてひとになることができる

ひとはうまれてからも
さまざまな臍帯とつながって
あたらしいひとになることができる

図書館は臍帯だ
さまざまなひとびとの智とつながって
ひとはあたらしいいのちを得る
きみが手にとることを待っている

書架に置かれた一冊の本が
手にした一冊の本が
きみをあたらしいひとに変えることがある

（編註）
南相馬市立中央図書館の依頼により書き下された作品。
二〇〇九年十二月から現在も、館内に直筆の色紙が額装され飾られている。

著者略歴

若松丈太郎（わかまつ　じょうたろう）

1935 年～ 2021 年。岩手県奥州市生まれ。福島大学卒業後、福島県浜通りの高等学校に国語教員として勤務。福島県南相馬市に暮らした。

著書：『若松丈太郎著作集　全三巻』（コールサック社）、詩集『夜の森』『夷俘の叛逆』など 11 冊、評論集『福島原発難民』『福島核災棄民』など 3 冊

翻訳者略歴

与那覇恵子（よなは　けいこ）

1953 年、沖縄県生まれ。沖縄県公立大学名桜大学元教授。英語翻訳・通訳者。

著書：詩集『沖縄から　見えるもの』、評論集『沖縄の怒り　政治的リテラシーを問う』、翻訳書『井上摩耶英日詩集　スモールワールド』（全てコールサック社）

郡山直（こおりやま　なおし）

1926 年、鹿児島県奄美の喜界島生まれ。東洋大学名誉教授。英語翻訳者。

著書：日本語詩集『詩人の引力』（コールサック社）、英語詩集『A FRESH LOAF OF POETRY FROM JAPAN』（学術研究出版）

若松丈太郎英日詩集　かなしみの土地
Jotaro Wakamatsu "Land of Sorrow"
A Collection of Poems in English and Japanese

2023 年 4 月 21 日　初版発行

著者　　　　　若松丈太郎
訳者　　　　　与那覇恵子　郡山直
編集・発行者　鈴木比佐雄
発行所　　　　株式会社 コールサック社
〒 173-0004　東京都板橋区板橋 2-63-4-209
電話 03-5944-3258　FAX 03-5944-3238
suzuki@coal-sack.com　http://www.coal-sack.com
郵便振替 00180-4-741802
印刷管理　（株）コールサック社　制作部

装丁　　松本菜央

落丁本・乱丁本はお取り替えいたします。
ISBN978-4-86435-564-3　C0092　￥2000E

Copyright © 2023 by Jotaro Wakamatsu
Translated by Keiko Yonaha, Naoshi Koriyama
Edited by Hisao Suzuki
Published by Coal Sack Publishing Company

Coal Sack Publishing Company
2-63-4-209 Itabashi Itabashi-ku Tokyo 173-0004 Japan
Tel: (03) 5944-3258 / Fax: (03) 5944-3238
suzuki@coal-sack.com　http://www.coal-sack.com
President: Hisao Suzuki

Land of Sorrow

A Collection of Poems
in English and Japanese

Jotaro Wakamatsu

Translated by Keiko Yonaha, Naoshi Koriyama

Translation was supervised by Meghan Kuckelman

Coal Sack Publishing Company
Tokyo, Japan

TABLE OF CONTENTS

Part 2: 15 Selected Poems

Translated by Naoshi Koriyama

INTRODUCTION
The Pride and Hope of "A highly persistent type of people"
by Hisao Suzuki

I published this English and Japanese anthology of poems, *Land of Sorrow*, wishing to send an encouraging message to the people of Japan and the world who deeply sympathize with the Ukrainian people still suffering in hardship.

Mr. Wakamatsu's wife, Ms. Yoko Wakamatsu, supported me by understanding the aim of the publication. I greatly appreciate it. Also, I'd like to deeply thank the translators, Ms. Keiko Yonaha and Mr. Naoshi Koriyama, and the supervising editor, Ms. Meghan Kuckelman, for their efforts. I want to explore the possibility that this analogy of poems can soon be interpreted in Ukrainian. In April 2021, the month after Mr. Wakamatsu passed away, I put my *in memoriam* poem in our literary magazine *Coal Sack*.

The Pride and Hope of "A highly persistent type of people"
A Monody for Jotaro Wakamatsu

At a checkpoint in a restricted zone 20 km from the Fukushima 1st Nuclear
Power Plant
many vehicles were refused entry, and they turned back.
You briefly talked with a policemen showing him your
"Haniya and Shimao Commemorative Literature Museum Researcher"
card, and they let us go.
Like a magic ticket,
the card opened the door to Odaka and Namie, "the Land of Sorrow."

April 10, 2011, ten years ago, a shopping arcade in front of the Odaka
railroad station,

turned into "The Town that Disappeared," which you had predicted.
Around the warped wire, only pigeons were flying in the cloudy sky.

At a drug store among a hundred shops lining the street,
you asked, "Do you know whose parents' house this is?"
When I couldn't answer,
you said, proudly, with a small smile,
"It's Yasuzo Suzuki's parents' house. He had a big influence on the Japanese
constitution."

Remembering the arcade in your hometown, Iwayado, Ōshū City in Iwate,
you talked about the literary history of the people in Odaka, with a population of only 10,000.
Your eyes were shining with hope,
a hope pushing the people trying to stand back up after the nuclear
accident.

I stood at the place again on May 3, 2021, ten years after the accident.
The drugstore had disappeared, no signboard, no warehouse, no store.
Even though the arcade is still missing some teeth,
some banks and stores have reopened.

At the party commemorating you in Minamisōma,
your two sons Masaki and Hiroki gave a speech,
saying that they respect and are proud of their father.
Your wife Yoko gave a speech,
saying that she appreciates and is proud of having been your wife.
Not seeking promotion, just as a teacher,
you listened to the words of your students in trouble.
Cherishing the local cultural activities and the literary people,
you were the core of the grassroots anti-nuclear power plant activity.
Your words in poems and criticism were the backbone of the people in

Japan.

In 1994, after retiring from teaching, you went to Chernobyl and
wrote the poem in *Land of Sorrow*, "The Town that Disappeared."
As a researcher at the Haniya and Shimao Commemorative Literature
  Museum,
you visited Yutaka Haniya and Toshio Shimao's wife Miho, and
asked them to donate their precious works to a local literature museum.
The editing was already finished on your research of many years,
a literary history of Fukushima Hamadōri,
called *A Highly Persistent Type of Family: The Sōma Region and Its
  Modern Literature.*
More than anything, your words were "a highly persistent type."
More than anything, your words were "the pride and hope of Fukushima
  Hamadōri,"
which will be handed down through this book and your poems.

Part 1:
Poems about the Nuclear Power Plants
of Ukraine and Fukushima

Translated by Keiko Yonaha

Land of Sorrow

"There will be no end to our suffering through generations."
Vladimir Romanenko, Director of the Ukraine National Research Center for Radiation Medicine

Prologue: Johan Apocalypse

About that day
and the following days,
St. John prophesized:
> From the sky, a big star like a burning torch will fall.
> The star will fall on one third of the rivers and springs.
> The name of the star is Chernobyl.
> One third of the water will be bitter
> and the bitter water will kill many people.*
Vladimir Shiroshitan, a chief of the Chernobyl International
    Center,
greeted us, "Welcome to the town of sorrow, Chernobyl."
In East Slav, the town's name means "wormwood."
Was it a town of sorrow from the start?
On April 26, 1986,
the Chernobyl Nuclear Power Plant No. 4 reactor exploded.
On that day
and on the following days
many people died
many people suffered and
many more people continue to suffer.

*Revelations 8: 10-11. Some of the words were changed without changing the basic meaning.

1. Butterfly a Hundred Years Ago

A twenty-five-year-old man killed himself before dawn today.
I glanced out the window of an Airbus A-310 gaining altitude
   after takeoff.
Recalling a hundred years ago today,
over the sea of clouds, the plane broke through.
I thought I saw a butterfly flying.
It must have been an illusion,
   but now, we are apart from each other in the East and the West.
   Looking back again and again, we are leaving.*
Early dawn thoughts of a man on May 16, 1894.
Pondering thoughts of a man on the same day, May 16, 1994.
Is there any bridge between them?
If there is, what is it?
What are they?
Are they butterflies?
Outside the window of the airbus,
tangling and dancing,
an illusion.

*Part of a work by Tokoku Kitamura, titled "So-cho no wakare."

2. Kyiv in May

Down is floating in the air of the old cobblestone street.
It is poplar down.
Horse chestnut trees with white flowers are in keeping with the
   cobblestone street.
They say Kyiv is the greenest city in Europe.

People are enjoying Vulycya Xreshatyk in May,
talking on the benches under the trees at night,
slowly walking the promenade under the trees.
I wonder if the uneven road shows us peoples' refracted minds.

At the bottom of the hill,
a Russian Orthodox church appears like the illusion of a border.
Joining the people,
we wander around the illusion
for the night view of the Dnieper River.

Visiting Mussorgsky's "La Grande Porte de Kyiv,"*
I remember the name of the poet that Ukrainians are proud of.
Horse chestnut flowers,
are they offered to Shevchenko?

*Modest Musorgskii, *Pictures at an Exhibition,* 1847.

3. Cutting off the Scenery

A border guard is talking on the phone
and the engine of our minibus cuts out.
It is found that our guide Vaya has left our papers behind.
Silence . . . like all the air is gone.
We try to relax outside
but we are ordered to stay close to the bus.
The ordinary road is blocked,
and it is a border
dividing Belarus and Ukraine.
Until 1991, the head of this road
and the tail of this road
were both in the USSR.
People were coming and going freely.
There is no line drawn on the road,
but the border is there,
blocked only by an ordinary pole
There is no line drawn on the road, but
imagining there is a line on the road,
I stand on it on one leg,
imitating the pose of a stork
trying to fly away,
imitating a scene from
a Theo Angelopoulos film.
The landscape in the movie was
full of rivers and lakes around the borders of
Greece, Albania and Yugoslavia,

and the low land of the Dnieper River branches,
spreading before the border of Ukraine and Belarus.
How similar they are!
With a puzzled face,
the border guard looks at me.
Can I fly from the pose of a stork
standing on the border on one leg?
A stork stands up. . .*
Sometimes storks make dangerous nests
on the tops of utility poles
or under a farmer's eaves.
In a village view like this,
Ukraine and Belarus share a C-shaped border
through which
an ordinary C-shaped road runs.
Less than ten kilometers of the road belongs to Belarus,
but each country has an immigration office at each border.
We humans draw territorial boundaries
on mountain ridges
on sand bars in rivers
on small islands in lakes
crossing the woods
crossing the fields
crossing the towns.
In front of the Brandenburg Gate,
when the angel from Wim Wenders's movie
crossed the border,
the black and white image shifted into color.*

Dividing this side and the other
the line that we have drawn on the map
runs in our hearts
so that
it divides us
it displaces us
and it makes targets of our bodies.
While we are forced to stay on the border,
a small truck piled up with milk cans
easily crosses
from Ukraine into Belarus
as if it were nothing,
together with radioactive materials
riding upon the winds,
just like a visionary butterfly.

A stork stands up: Theo Angelopoulos. *To Meteoro Vima Tu Pelargu*, 1991, film, Greece.
the black and white image shifted into color: Wim Wenders. *Wings of Desire*, 1988, film, West German and France.

4. Reviving an Evil Spirit

Right before my eyes is the
Chernobyl Nuclear Power Plant Furnace No. 4
which I have seen many times,
but only in photos.
A sarcophagus,

evil-looking and ill-omened.
The evil spirit of Hades was shut in
with 500,000m³ of concrete and 6,000 tons of iron.
Now that evil spirit is about to revive.
The dosimeter's needle
is off the scale,
proving that the air of evil
is unmeasurable.
"You can only stay five minutes,"
the guide says.
An asphalt square and
an observatory for viewing a sarcophagus—
no, it's an altar for burning incense.
Contaminants lay buried under our feet.
No, I don't want to stay here,
not even for five minutes.
No pain,
but already we are contaminated.
Painful red rust peels
from the damaged steel wreckage.
Here in this bleak landscape
everything is exposed to the weather
and to the blowing wind.
Here in this contaminated forest
the leaves have turned red.
Unseasonable, they say.
A carrot-colored forest,
a symbol of people's fears,

cut and buried,
a forest empty of trees.
All of us are witnessing
bleak and desolate nature.

5. Exposing Myself to Death

On the border of Chernobyl's 30-km Zone, there is a gate. From next to the gate, an endlessly shabby iron wire fence restricts the exclusion zone. Until now, rich, beautiful green fields of grain had been spreading before our eyes. However, inside the fence in the barrier field, only withered red grass stands lonely and bored.

While we were waiting for the bus to pick us up, three buses came from Kyiv, and the passengers changed to a new bus. Probably they changed their bus from a non-contaminated one to a contaminated one at the gate. Men and women, passengers of different ages, are working at the Chernobyl Nuclear Power Plant. They said that they work by alternating every two weeks at the plant and its related facilities.

The 30-km Zone is a restricted area; however, it seems that many more people than I thought are working here to earn their living. Furnaces No. 1, 2, and 3 are still working even though they are adjacent to Furnace No. 4, the one involved in the accident. The Zone also includes the International Academy Research Center where we heard an explanation and had lunch. There, I heard there were other research facilities as well. From the bus, I saw people fishing in the man-made pond when we passed near Furnaces No. 5 and 6. It's just for amusement during lunch, they

say, but, still, it surprised me that they freely enjoy fishing in a contaminated man-made pond. I don't think they eat what they catch, but even so, it was a surprise to me. At the observatory in Furnace No. 4, the dosimeter that I brought pushed its counter to the limit and we became restless. However, workers there were passing by us as if nothing was happening. It was an unmarried lady who guided us inside the Zone on a bus. Given that she is going to have a baby someday, she should not work here, but she said that she was working here with that in her mind. Out of the bus window, we saw abandoned farmhouses, livestock barns, leggy fruit tree branches, and an old tractor track on a path in a nearby field. They were heart-breaking scenes.

Among the farmers forced to leave, some have returned and live in their villages, mostly old people who are overlooked. Among the people of Pearl Chef Village, which 350 families left, at most 170 people have returned and only 109 people are living there now. One of them is 78-year-old Maarja Pulica. Before the accident, she lost her husband, and during the evacuation, she had to live with two drunk men in an apartment-like place. Unable to bear that situation, she returned to her home three months later. She told us that she was not afraid of dying since she was old enough. It is natural for ordinary people to not be able to maintain their ordinary lives in times of emergency. In order to live their lives, ordinary people have to expose themselves to death.

6. The Town that Disappeared

Within two hours, forty-five thousand people disappeared,

but not like leaving a stadium after enjoying a soccer game.
Whole, ordinary lives were just spirited away from the town.
The radio issued the evacuation alarm:
"Please pack food for three days."
Thinking they could come back after three days,
most people left their homes
with only small shopping bags.
An old lady holding only a kitten in her arms,
sick people in the hospitals,
all forty-five thousand people, gone in two hours,
boarding eleven hundred buses.
The cries of children playing tag,
the greetings of neighbors over the fence,
the ringing bell of a postman on a bicycle,
the good smells of simmering borsch,
lights in the windows of the houses at night—
people's daily lives were gone.
The city of Pripyat disappeared from the map.
Everything happened in the forty hours after
the accident at the Chernobyl Nuclear Power Plant.
People from Pripyat scattered, boarding
eleven hundred buses in two hours.
Including three neighboring villages, forty-nine thousand people
    were spirited away.
Forty-nine thousand is the population of Haramachi City,
where I live.
Centered around the Chernobyl Nuclear Power Plant,
a radius of thirty kilometers was designated as a danger zone.

Over three days starting May 6, the eleventh day after the accident,
ninety-two thousand more, totaling about one hundred fifty thousand people,
dispersed to
farm villages one hundred or one hundred fifty kilometers away.
Centered around the Fukushima Nuclear Power Plant,
a zone with a radius of thirty kilometers would include
the cities of Futaba, Okuma, Tomioka, Naraha, Namie,
Hirono, the villages of Kawauchi, Miyakoji, Katurao,
Odaka City, the northern part of Iwaki City,
and my hometown, Haramachi City.
Here in that zone in Japan,
about one hundred fifty thousand people live.
Where could we disperse to?
Where could we hide?
Some villages still had an evacuation order
six years after the Chernobyl accident.
We enter the city of Pripyat in the eighth year
after the accident.
Weeds emerge out of the cracked pavement,
opening the cracks wider.
Swallows swoop by.
Pigeons inflate their breasts.
Butterflies rest on flowers.
Flies buzz about.
Mosquitoes swarm into a rotating column.
Leaves from the roadside trees surrender to the wind.
However,

no human voice calls out in the town.
No human walks the street.
Forty-five thousand people are playing hide and seek.
I, being "it," am looking for them.
"Ready or not, here I come."
A toy left behind in the hallway of a nursery school,
a stew pot abandoned on a burner in a kitchen,
papers spread out on desks,
everywhere, I feel that someone existed
until just a few moments ago.
The sun is setting already
and I'm "it," at a loss,
standing alone in the plaza.
Friends are all gone,
taken by an evil spirit.
The hotel, department stores,
the cultural centers, school buildings,
apartments buildings—
all have started to crumble.
Everything moves toward "ruin."
The lives of the people
and the city that the people built
compete to see which can fall to ruin faster.

 Strontium 90: half-life 29 years.
 Caesium 137: half-life 30 years.
 Plutonium 239: half-life 24,000 years.
Ninety years for Caesium to decrease to one-eighth.
Eight times more Caesium than the lethal dose

will continue to kill for ninety years.
Humans cannot control what they did one hundred years ago.
Then,
isn't it impudent for humans to play with plutonium?
Walking through the abandoned hall of a nursing school,
I set my foot in some weeds.
I'm afraid I may have disturbed some radioactive particles
and my lungs have already taken some in
with the air I breathed.
I'm sure
more cities will disappear
from the earth.
Today may be the day
that we disappear.
I think I hear a child's call.
Turning, I see nobody behind me.
A chill runs down my spine.
Alone, I'm just standing still
here in the plaza.

7. Captives

Having met the children hospitalized in the hospital affiliated with the Kyiv Research Institute of Pediatrics, Obstetrics and Gynecology, I felt that the children of Ukraine and Belarus were captives. They looked like they were concentrating on the conversation between doctors and us foreigners in order to get information about the unreasonable situation that they are forced to live in.

You know, sometimes children can understand things more deeply than adults and get to the point of the truth. Watching them, I thought about Florya and Glasha, children a half-century ago. They are a boy and a girl from a small village in Belarus on the upper Dnieper in the movie *Come and See* (Japanese title: *Flame/628*)* which brought accusations against Nazi crimes committed in the village in 1943. Once, I wrote about these two children, Florya and Glasha, in my poem "In Winter."*

*Elem Germanovich Limoz. *Come and See*, 1985, film, USSR.
*88 *Fukushima Prefecture Collection of Modern Poems*, first publication.

In Winter
To the north,
at the end of December,
I saw only
withered trees,
a landscape soaked in fixing solution,
imagination weakened by cataracts.
Isn't there anything that will start to move?
At a small station on the way,
a girl slightly limping on her left leg got on the train
and sat in front of me.
She looked like Glasha,
in her high cheek bones,
in her eyes and lips.
A white whistle in her mouth,
she is coming down the hill

with a bloody inner thigh.
Toward Florya, she comes limping.
Since Florya saw too much of human history
and the whole world,
he had too many wrinkles on his forehead
for his age,
living in the village of Hatieni in Byelorussia
in 1943.
Since 1945,
he had lost what he should really believe.
Maybe I myself, too.
As if they had no place to go,
like drifting leaves,
young people crowded themselves in the corner of the street.
I bought a collection of poems.
Wasn't it the village on the leeward side of Chernobyl
in April 1986?
At night
I used a loupe to look for the people
in the new year's calendar spread on the floor.
January, Saint Moritz, nobody.
February, Luzern, nobody.
When can I see somebody?
March, Zermatt, nobody.
April, Montord—
I thought I saw a figure like a human
crouching down on a pier of Lake Le Mans.

Even with my acknowledgement that Florya's facial expression was made by an actor in the movie, I still cannot forget it. No other century has been treating children as cruelly as this century, especially the latter half of this century. Not only indiscriminate attacks, nuclear bombs, massacres in concentration camps, but also mean-spirited staff in our daily life. I wonder what this century will relegate to children in the next century. I ended up feeling that all children might be captives, having met the children hospitalized in the hospital attached to the Ukraine National Center for Radiation Medicine.

8. The Flow of Bitter Water

Melting the winter snow and
gathering blessed water from heaven,
in May, tributaries of the Dnieper River
cross the natural embankment,
swell and overflow
as far as we can see,
like rice fields just finished planting.
Fertile soil is matured
with rich water.
The Dnieper basin is vast.
Having not only Ukraine
but also Russia and Belarus
as its water sources,
the Pripyat River joins
at the place

where Chernobyl lies.
On the map showing the areas contaminated by Caesium 137,
around a third of the river upstream was colored,
meaning that bitter water was pushed into the river.
Within an area ten kilometers around Chernobyl,
under the earthen mounds where wormwood thickly grows,
under the eight hundred earthen mounds,
polluted materials are buried.
Eight hundred earthen mounds turn
underground water into bitter water.
They say that
the sarcophagus has started to crack.
They say that
the condition of the ground is critical
due to the heat and weight.
From the man-made pond of the nuclear power plant,
water flows into the Pripyat River,
the Pripyat flows into the Dnieper,
and the water-rich Dnieper flows
with the bitter water itself.

9. A Water Planet Sleeping in a White Aqua

Wrapped in a thick film of water vapor,
a water planet sinks under my eyes.
My lonely flight to the East
left Moscow at eight p.m.
With the sun on the left,

it feels like time has stopped,
like I'm floating.
Here, we have a white night,
and the setting sun starts to shed the morning sunlight
at the same time.
I imagine a river running
on the surface of the earth
on a dark stagnant night.
I imagine
people sinking into sleep for a brief time
before the night breaks.
I wonder
if butterflies are dancing in their dreams.
No butterflies
outside the window.

Epilogue: A Shape of Sorrow

At an exhibition of "National Treasures, Horyu-ji Temple" held at the Tokyo
National Museum

Seeing the statue of Nikko Bosatu (Bodhisattva)
I thought of the children in Ukraine.
I realized, all the more, that
there is no difference between
grief 1,000 years ago
and grief today.
What we experienced in the past
will be scheduled in the future.

Tears overflow my eyes.
Water overflows the Dnieper River.
The bitter water overflows the dam of the Dnieper River.

Notes: These nine poems were written after having joined the Fukushima prefecture citizens' survey tour of Chernobyl.

References
Matuoka Nobuo. *Documentary Chernobyl*, 1988, Ryokufu Shuppan.
Hirokawa Ryuichi. *Chernobyl Report*, 1991, Iwanami Shoten.
Alla Yaroshinskaya. *Chernobyl Top Secret*, 1994, Heibon-sha.

Editorial notes
"Prologue: Johan Apocalypse" was changed to "I Johan Apocalypse" in the collection of poems titled *There, Many Rivers Run*, and "Butterfly a Hundred Years Ago" and "Epilogue: A Shape of Sorrow" were not included in that collection. *The Land of Sorrow* in the anthology *Elegy* (1994, Dorinsha) is found in this book. *130 Selected Poems of Wakamatsu Jotaro* (2014, Coal Sack) contains its original version.

There, Many Rivers Run

Let us see the Dnieper River at night.
Going up a dark hill,
going down another hill with only a little light,
Saint Andrew's Church bursts suddenly
upon my sight.
From the church to the night street of the dead,
I wander around at night.
Let us wander.
Did I wander around the hill of Vladimir?
Did I wander around the park of Pioneeru?
The further I wander around the night street of the dead,
the further away the Dnieper River becomes.
The width of the invisible Dnieper increases.
The water of the invisible Dnieper increases.
Swallowed by the dark,
I surrender myself to
the tour of the womb.
Let me wander around.
What lured me to the tour of the night river?
If I had found the way to the path
to the riverbank,
would I also have found myself drifting away
along the dark surface of the river?

The light and shadow ripples in the pond

in the courtyard of al Beerkah,
reflects on the wall of al Berkah.

When I was blankly gazing at the fluctuation of light
and shadow on the wall of Alhambra, a man in his forties
spoke to me, asking, "Are you Japanese?"

He said that he had been living here in Finland for
twenty years after marrying a local woman. He pointed at
the woman standing a little way away, saying "I'm with her."

When I told him that my wife traveled around Finland
and the Baltic states the year before and came to love the
countries very much, he said, "That's good."

The debris of Japanese words scattered around us and
the sunlight through the leaves of the trees rested on them.

Is it too much to say that I felt some sorrow in his back
as he left?

Light and shadow created by the water of al Beerkah
reflects on the wall of al Berkah
One of the "e's" hid itself somewhere.
Is only the sound of the "e" hidden?
The man also hid himself in the shadow of the wall
of al Beerkah together with his Finnish wife.
Light and shadow reflects on the wall of al Berkah.
Blankly, I gaze as it flickers.

Poplar down is drifting around Europe in May
from the sky over the fields of Ukraine

to Prague and Kulakov
to Belgrade and Sarajevo.
Bearing tiny seeds,
summer snow is drifting about.

The Earth is strewn with land mines.
In May poplar down drifts over the minefields
bearing tiny seeds for the Earth,
bearing radioactive materials on a whim.
It seems as if,
when the land mines explode,
the earth itself explodes.

In March 1999, I was traveling around the Danube River basin and on the 24th I was in Bratislava. That night, a NATO air strike hit Belgrade five hundred kilometers away. The next morning, on the 25th, the phrase "Europe at War" jumped out at me from the TV. I heard that security checks were tightening at the Danube River border crossing into Komarom, Hungary, from Komarno, Slovakia, especially for people traveling alone. At the same time, it looked like local people were coming and going as usual across the border bridge by bike, by car or on foot. Even though they belong to different countries, Komarom and Komarno are neighboring towns across from each other on the Danube River. On the 27th, the security check was further tightened at the border of Klingenbach, Austria, and Sopron, Hungary. A border guard got on the bus and checked us one by one,

comparing our passport photos and our faces. He even checked the contents of the luggage compartment. The borders in Europe were in a tense state. On the 26th, I got a newspaper in Magyar at the subway station in Budapest. The headline over the top article read, "A NATO Kitartoan Bambaz." I tried to grasp the situation, picking up words such as Belgrade, Kuld, Yugoslavia, Milošević, and Bambaztak. Budapest is three hundred kilometers away from Belgrade. On the afternoon on the 28th, Serbian people gathered for an anti-NATO protest in Heldenplatz in Vienna. It was just before nine o'clock at night, and I again came across them marching in a demonstration. Going back to my hotel facing the Danube River, I got off the No. 21 streetcar and looked up at Mars emitting a strong light of ill-omened blood in the sky above the dark Danube River, which absorbs everything as it flows. The Danube River runs from Vienna to Bratislava, Dunakanyar and Budapest, where I traveled. Further down, it reaches Belgrade where I suppose the air attacks are still going on tonight.

The sea cactus gives off a green light when touched.
It's the same with the firefly squid and, of course, the firefly.
Luminous creatures are beautiful and sorrowful,
including our own luminous earth.

In the evening
the telephone rang, "brrring."

Is this Mr. Wago? No?
I heard the voice of an old friend whom I hadn't seen for thirty
    years.
Oh? Is this Non-chan?
Is it you? Non-chan?

Butcherbirds have nested in a hole in the pillar of my veranda.
Maybe there are baby birds.
Parent birds busily come and go.
Dandelion down drifts about busily.
My neighbor's grandchild is shouting aloud.
Their daughter returned home with her child
to take care of her mother who'd had surgery for a brain tumor.
It was highly humid yesterday.
Today it is dry and cool.

    In Jerez de la Frontera
    we can see water and shadow,
    shadow and water.
    I wonder if that was what Lorca said.

FEDERICO GARCÍA LORCA
Each name hides "RC" in it.
Did you know that?
Sure, Lorca knows it.
What does "RC" mean to Lorca?
What does "RC" mean to the world?
Where is the olive grove where Lorca was killed?

Where is the olive grove where Lorca's body was hidden?

A bus goes through the stony grove.
No grass grows in the gravelly soil.
I know the earth has so much of this gravelly soil.
From the bottom of such a landscape
I thought I heard the sound of water.
The murmur of the brook that I heard,
was it my auditory hallucination?
People's conversations that I heard,
were they my auditory hallucination?
The earth has much gravelly soil where no grass grows.

Over there,
in a landscape cut by a mountain ridge,
a cloth bundle appears,
followed by the head that holds up the bundle.
Then, there appears the torso
that holds up the head
that holds up the bundle,
till finally, the whole body comes into view.
A man with all his household goods on his head
slowly approaches alone.
Behind him
invisible
tens of thousands of people keep on walking
without a destination.
Sitting on the roadside,

I have nothing to do but watch them walk by.
I'm just watching these people
walking without a destination.
The earth has much gravelly soil where no grass grows.
Into such soil
soaks their blood.

      The town covered with falling snow is located on sloping ground. When I first viewed the town from the top of the postroad, I realized that I had been waited for by a man who lived there and died there.

      He waited for me sitting on a chair at a store front. He spent all day waiting for me to appear at the top of the postroad and slowly come down to notice him and call out to him.

      Such a day repeated for years.

      During these years, I never stood on the top of the hill and never slowly walked down to call on him.

      The man died.

      On the day of his funeral, the falling snow covered the postroad of the town.

      For the first time, I stood on the top of the white hill.

      I realized that I came to this white town too late.

What was there?
What was not there?
and
What is going to be there?

What did you do?
What did you not do?
and
What are you going to do?

Over there at the sea,
the telephone rings, "brrring, brrring."
Who is calling?
Mud and water
as far as I can see.
An alluvial plain spreading at the mouth of the river,
viewed from the height of the atmosphere.
As far as the visible edge
just mud and water.

As far as the visible edge
nothing but mud and water,
no sign of the living.
Is it a world of beginning?
Is it a world of ending?
Quietly, just mud and water.

Far up the river, on the banks of the tributary named
the Bagmati River, the Pashupatinath Temple stands.
Hindus bathe at waterside ghats in the morning, wash in
the afternoon, and are cremated at Arya Ghat in the evening. The Bagmati River carries away Hindus' bones, ashes,

dirt, and waste, all the proof of having lived gone down-stream. On the shores upriver, Lamaists' prayer flags flutter in the wind. Collecting many tributaries, the banks of the great river Ganges are filled with many different kinds of people. Buddhists burn incense. Christians receive the Sacraments. Muslims recite Scripture. The Ganges swallows people's bones, ashes, dirt, and waste, all the proof of having lived, and carries it downstream to the alluvial plain spread at the mouth of river.

In the shallow stream of the Bagmati River
a piece of firewood got caught.
In the crematorium in the Pashupatinath Temple
the flames and smoke of cremation drift up to the sky,
while bones and ashes go down to the shallow stream of the
   Bagmati River

The Naruse River rapids roar loudly.
The river's other name is Hitokabe.
Going back into a V-shaped valley,
it reaches my mother's hometown, Yonezato village, Hitokabe.
Hitokabe.
My illusory Heimat.
Since there is a place called Onikabe—*demon head*—
it's no wonder that there is a place called Hitokabe—*human head*.
From Hitokabe,
crossing over the Ubaishi ridge,
just like wandering around a dark night path in the underworld.

Ozaki
Ashizaki—*cape of leg*
Kubizaki—*cape of neck*
Should I reach
Shikotsu Zaki—*cape of dead bones?*
Should a wanderer also be washed ashore?
Everything was washed up on the shore.

So
What was there?
and
What was not there?
chaos of mud and water
chaos of mud and water
I sink into it,
seeking something to sympathize with.

In the mud and water
I am decomposed. Mud and water permeate me.
I am now mud and water

Can I, mud and water,
create
something?

boundless water
shine repelling light
boundless mud

shine repelling light

light and shadow
water and shadow
shadow and water
mud and water

Brrring, brrring.
Someone's phone rings somewhere.
The phone nobody picks up
keeps on ringing
vibrating the air
forever
and ever.

A Person Who Deeply Cares about "Captives": Reading the Eleven Poems of *Land of Sorrow*
by Hisao Suzuki

1.

The *Jotaro Wakamatsu Collection in Three Volumes* was first pub-lished in Japanese in early March 2022, the month before the first anniver-sary of his death. The most well-known poem, "The Town that Disappeared," is one of eleven poems in *Land of Sorrow*; however, as far as I know, it seems that the rest of the ten poems were not much discussed, and the whole picture of the eleven poems and their message was hardly reported. I wanted to discuss *Land of Sorrow* when I had a chance to talk about Wakamatsu. Understanding these poems led me to convey the poet's message.

The Russian Army invaded Ukraine on the 26th of February, 2022. The news that shook the world was that before heading to Kyiv, the Russian Army occupied the Chernobyl Nuclear Power Plant and built a trench in the "red forest," still contaminated by radioactive material. Jotaro Wakamatsu, who passed away in April 2021, visited Kyiv in April 1994. I wondered what he would have said if he had heard the news. After the Russian inva-sion, the Ukrainian Army turned to attack the Russian Army in May, and Russia withdrew from the Chernobyl Nuclear Power Plant. In the reporting on that situation in Japan, it was announced that the pronunciation of the foreign place names was being changed to reflect the Ukranian pronuncia-tion instead of the Russian pronunciation, for example, "Cheruno-Biri" for "Cherunobuiri" (Chernobyl) and "Ki-u" for "Kiefu" (Kyiv). I also won-dered how Wakamatsu would have written about it in his writings if he had heard it. It is a great shame that I cannot read anymore of his new writings now, and when I realized that as a poet and a critic, he was the only pre-cious person who could tell of the tragedy of Nuclear Power Plants to the world, I suffered a greater sense of loss at his death. The eleven poems in

Land of Sorrow deepen his message by showing the people, movies and writings that affected him, which is just like a symphony composed of eleven poems telling of the fate of Chernobyl.

Wakamatsu used Revelations 8:10-11 from the Bible in "Prologue: Johan Apocalypse."

> St. John prophesized:
>> From the sky, a big star like a burning torch will fall.
>> The star will fall on one third of the rivers and springs.
>> The name of the star is Chernobyl.
>> One third of the water will be bitter
>> and the bitter water will kill many people.

Why did he start with St. John's prophecy that "From the sky, a big star like a burning torch will fall"? A nuclear power plant accident is a nuclear explosion, and it is just like "a big star like a burning torch" falling to the earth. That "Chernobyl" means "wormwood" in East Slav implies that this place is cursed.

> Vladimir Shiroshitan, a chief of the Chernobyl International Center, greeted us, "Welcome to the town of sorrow, Chernobyl."
> In East Slav, the town's name means "wormwood."
> Was it a town of sorrow from the start?

Vladimir Shiroshitan's greeting, "Welcome to the town of sorrow, Chernobyl," impressed Wakamatsu, and being inspired by its sound and meaning, it seems that the seed of a series of poems, *Land of Sorrow*, was planted at that time.

In "Butterfly a Hundred Years Ago," he imagines a butterfly flying over a sea of clouds out of the window of an airplane to Russia and Ukraine.

> I thought I saw a butterfly flying.
> It must have been an illusion, but
> now, we are apart from each other in the East and the West.
> Looking back again and again, we are leaving.
> Early dawn thoughts of a man on May 16, 1894.
> Pondering thoughts of a man on the same day, May 16, 1994.

Is there any bridge between them?

Quoting "So-Cho no Wakare" (farewell of a pair of butterflies), a poem by Tokoku Kitamura, who committed suicide one hundred years ago on May 16, Wakamatsu thinks about the poet who created the starting point for modern Japanese poetry and poetry criticism. I think he may have wanted the willpower Kitamura expresses in his lyrics and his representative essay on poetry, "Naibu Seimei Ron" ("Theory of Inner Life"). On May 16, one hundred years ago, Kitamura took his own life, seeking the importance of altruism, pacifism, and internalization. It happened to be the same day of May 16, one hundred years later, when Wakamatsu left for Chernobyl in Ukraine, the place suffering from radioactive contamination. In a way, Wakamatsu may have found a similarity between Kitamura's leaving for another world and his own leaving for the other world of Chernobyl. Out of the window, he may have imagined a butterfly as an avatar for Kitamura. In "Kyiv in May," praising Kyiv's scenery, he writes about a popular Ukrainian poet and a famous Russian composer.

> Down is floating in the air of the old cobblestone street.
> It is poplar down.
> Horse chestnut trees with white flowers are in keeping with the
>   cobblestone street.
> They say Kyiv is the greenest city in Europe.
> People are enjoying Vulycya Xreshatyk in May,

Wakamatsu describes the poplar down floating in the street of Kyiv, the people walking amid rows of horse chestnuts, and how they enjoy and love their town, Kyiv. He also writes, "I wonder if the uneven road shows us peoples' refracted minds" and considers their history of hardship. By citing two artists, he writes about the old city of art.

> Visiting Mussorgsky's "La Grande Porte de Kyiv,"
> I remember the name of the poet that Ukrainians are proud of.
> Horse chestnut flowers,
>   are they offered to Shevchenko?

Russian composer Mussorgsky's "La Grande Porte de Kyiv" in *Pictures at*

an *Exhibition*, consoling his friend's soul, is a masterpiece you will never forget once you listen to it. Wakamatsu visited the "La Grande Porte de Kyiv." Taras Shevchenko is a Ukrainian poet famous for "Kobzar," written not in Russian but in Ukrainian for the first time. He is also an artist renowned for a series of paintings. In it, the sad face and lowered eyes of "Kateryna," a daughter being toyed with by a Russian officer, is incredibly touching. Wakamatsu's words, "Horse chestnut flowers, / are they offered to Shevchenko?" tells that he must have been impressed with Ukrainian people, who have shown their pride in the nineteenth-century poet Shevchenko by erecting a bronze statue of him.

In "Cutting off the Scenery," Wakamatsu witnesses a tense atmosphere that reminds him of the border scenes in two movies: *To Meteoro Vima Tu Pelargu*, a 1991 Greek film by Theo Angelopoulos, and *Wings of Desire*, a 1988 Wim Wenders film out of West Germany and France. Even though Wakamatsu's poems are mainly about Fukushima and Tohoku, we see global views in his poems from the influence of the foreign movies he watched from his college days to his death. Witnessing the Ukrainian border with Belarus and Russia, he wrote these lines.

> imitating a scene from
> a Theo Angelopoulos film.
> The landscape in the movie was
> full of rivers and lakes around the borders of
> Greece, Albania and Yugoslavia,
> and the low land of the Dnieper River branches,
> spreading before the border of Ukraine and Belarus.
> How similar they are!
> With a puzzled face,
> the border guard looks at me.
> Can I fly from the pose of a stork
> standing on the border on one leg?
> A stork stands up. . .
> […]

> [The border] divides us
> it displaces us
> and it makes targets of our bodies.
> While we are forced to stay on the border,
> a small truck piled up with milk cans
> easily crosses
> from Ukraine into Belarus
> as if it were nothing,
> together with radioactive materials
> riding upon the winds,
> just like a visionary butterfly.

In April 1994, like a prophecy, through these lines, Wakamatsu visualized the scene of displacement perpetuated when the Russian Army invaded Ukraine by crossing the border from Belarus on February 26, 2022.

"The Town that Disappeared" seems to predict the Fukushima Nuclear Power Plant accident, and I feel that Wakamatsu predicted Russia's invasion in the lines of "Cutting off the Scenery." If he were alive, he would have written more poems and essays filled with fierce anger about having predicted the actions of idiotic humans who repeatedly trump other countries by crossing the borders.

"Reviving an Evil Spirit" tells of his shock when he saw the sarcophagus of the Chernobyl Nuclear Power plant Furnace No. 4 reactor. In a way, Wakamatsu's predictive words may bespeak the worst ending caused by humanity's cursed evil spirit:

> Right before my eyes is the
> Chernobyl Nuclear Power Plant Furnace No. 4
> which I have seen many times,
> but only in photos.
> A sarcophagus,
> evil-looking and ill-omened.
> The evil spirit of Hades was shut in
> with 500,000m^3 of concrete and 6,000 tons of iron.

Now that evil spirit is about to revive.
The dosimeter's needle
is off the scale,
proving that the air of evil
is unmeasurable.
"You can only stay five minutes,"
the guide says.
An asphalt square and
an observatory for viewing a sarcophagus—
no, it's an altar for burning incense.
Contaminants lay buried under our feet.
No, I don't want to stay here,
not even for five minutes.
No pain,
but already we are contaminated.

Probably, Wakamatsu's trip aimed to face the stark reality of the sarcophagus, the living evil spirit. The dosimeter's needle was off the scale, showing that the air of evil is unmeasurable, and though he was told that he could stay for five minutes, he wanted to run away as soon as possible. He was terrified to feel radioactive material rushing toward them to contaminate them. His aim for the trip was realized since he could describe this terrifying fear even eight years after the accident. The evil spirit fell onto the forest, making it appear a "carrot-colored forest," symbolizing people's fears. It is said that the evil spirit was cut down and buried. However, in 2022 Russian officers ordered the soldiers to dig out the "carrot-colored forest" for their trenches, which contaminated these soldiers with radioactivity. It was found that the tragedy of Chernobyl was not previously known to the Russian soldiers.

"Exposing Myself to Death" describes the daily life of Chernobyl's 30-km Zone after the accident.

On the border of Chernobyl's 30-km Zone, there is a gate.
From next to the gate, an endlessly shabby iron wire fence restricts

the exclusion zone. Until now, rich, beautiful green fields of grain had been spreading before our eyes. However, inside the fence in the barrier field, only withered red grass stands lonely and bored.

While we were waiting for the bus to pick us up, three buses came from Kyiv, and the passengers changed to a new bus. Probably they changed their bus from a non-contaminated one to a contaminated one at the gate. Men and women, passengers of different ages, are working at the Chernobyl Nuclear Power Plant. They said that they work by alternating every two weeks at the plant and its related facilities.

The 30-km Zone is a restricted area; however, it seems that many more people than I thought are working here to earn their living. Furnaces No. 1, 2, and 3 are still working even though they are adjacent to Furnace No. 4, the one involved in the accident. The Zone also includes the International Academy Research Center where we heard an explanation and had lunch. There, I heard there were other research facilities as well. From the bus, I saw people fishing in the man-made pond when we passed near Furnaces No. 5 and 6. It's just for amusement during lunch, they say, but, still, it surprised me that they freely enjoy fishing in a contaminated man-made pond. I don't think they eat what they catch, but even so, it was a surprise to me. At the observatory in Furnace No.4, the dosimeter that I brought pushed its counter to the limit and we became restless. However, workers there were passing by us as if nothing was happening. It was an unmarried lady who guided us inside the Zone on a bus. Given that she is going to have a baby someday, she should not work here, but she said that she was working here with that in her mind.

Wakamatsu found that people working at the power plant and related facilities for two-week shifts exchanged buses between the inside and outside of the contaminated off-limits area of Chernobyl's 30-km Zone. He also found, to his surprise, that nearby the destroyed Furnace No. 4, workers

enjoyed fishing in the artificial pond, and a bus guide in the zone is an unmarried young woman, which deepens his worry that the radiation risk
measures are not enough. He also introduces the older people who returned
to their homes and lives, exposing themselves to death. Finding the world
eight years after the accident, he could not have helped imagining a similar
situation involving the Fukushima Nuclear Power Plant's own 30-km
Zone, which included his hometown Haramachi City, which later became
Minamisōma City after a merger with Odaka City. I suppose that by de-
scribing the people working in nuclear power plants and related facilities,
and old people returning to their homes in Chernobyl's 30-km Zone, the
following image of "The Town that Disappeared" emerged.

2.
    Writing "The Town that Disappeared" required the indispensable ex-
perience in the first five poems, in addition to the prologue touched with the
word "wormwood" in Johan Apocalypse. Wakamatsu applied the experi-
ence of Chernobyl to the Fukushima No. 1 Nuclear Power Plant:
        People from Pripyat scattered, boarding
        eleven hundred buses in two hours.
        Including three neighboring villages, forty-nine thousand people
            were spirited away.
        Forty-nine thousand is the population of Haramachi City,
        where I live.
        Centered around the Chernobyl Nuclear Power Plant,
        a radius of thirty kilometers was designated as a danger zone.
        Over three days starting May 6, the eleventh day after the accident,
        ninety-two thousand more, totaling about one hundred fifty thou-
            sand people,
        dispersed to
        farm villages one hundred or one hundred fifty kilometers away.
        Centered around the Fukushima Nuclear Power Plant,
        a zone with a radius of thirty kilometers would include

the cities of Futaba, Okuma, Tomioka, Naraha, Namie,
Hirono, the villages of Kawauchi, Miyakoji, Katurao,
Odaka City, the northern part of Iwaki City,
and my hometown, Haramachi City.
Here in that zone in Japan,
about one hundred fifty thousand people live.
Where could we disperse to?
Where could we hide?
Some villages still had an evacuation order
six years after the Chernobyl accident.
We enter the city of Pripyat in the eighth year
after the accident.

Finding that "Haramachi City / where I live" has about the same population
of forty-nine thousand as that of "Pripyat City," he was attacked by the fear
that the same thing would happen to Haramachi in the near future. It was
also found that the population of one hundred fifty thousand in Chernobyl's
30-km Zone is the same as that of Fukushima's 30-km Zone. Wakamatsu
may have had a poetic imagination that could see people and cities in the
future from a universal view through the similarity of demographic statis-
tics and a broad geological sense. He did not like the expression "prediction," like "he predicted the nuclear power plant accident." Rejecting the
word "prediction," he said, "I wrote just what I felt, and it came from only
the facts I accumulated." We should refer to his interview with the photog-
rapher Mr. Kazuto Sugita in "Interview and Dialogue, " chapter 3 of volume 2 of Wakamatsu's book collection, *Kyokutan Nebarizoku no Keifu (A
Highly Persistent Type of Family)*. He answered Kazuto's question with,
"When I write a poem, I express what I feel through my sense rather than
what I think in my head, even if it is invisible and inaudible. " His uncom-
fortable feeling toward the word "prediction" or "foreknowledge" seems to
come from the attitude of seeing the invisible and hearing the inaudible.

The poem "Captives" tells us of his feelings when he met the children
exposed to radiation at the Kyiv Pediatrics and ObGyn research hospital.

Having met the children hospitalized in the hospital affiliated with the Kyiv Research Institute of Pediatrics, Obstetrics and Gynecology, I felt that the children of Ukraine and Belarus were captives. They looked like they were concentrating on the conversation between doctors and us foreigners in order to get information about the unreasonable situation that they are forced to live in. You know, sometimes children can understand things more deeply than adults and get to the point of the truth. Watching them, I thought about Florya and Glasha, children a half-century ago. In the movie *Come and See* they are a boy and girl from a small village in Belarus on the upper Dnieper who, in 1943, bring accusations against Nazi crimes. Once, I wrote about these two children, Florya and Glasha, in my poem "In Winter."

Wakamatsu seems to have found that "children can understand things more deeply than adults and get to the point of the truth" about the situation where they were put through the questions asked by the Japanese. These children reminded him of the Russia/Belarus movie *Come and See*, directed by Elem Germanovich. In the movie, a boy from Belarus enters the Soviet partisans forces in order to protect his village; however, he witnesses German Nazis raping and killing all the people of 628 villages. Witnessing all these continuous massacres, the face of the boy turned into the face of an older man by the end of the film. Wakamatsu saw the face of the boy Florya in those of the children under treatment in the hospital and was gravely worried about the future of these children suffering from diseases, and yet still trying to have hope.

"The Flow of Bitter Water" describes the situation from the poem "Prologue: Johan Apocalypse," in which "One third of the water will be bitter, and the bitter water will kill many people." This became a reality in the 21st century:

> The Dnieper basin is vast.
> Having not only Ukraine
> but also Russia and Belarus

as its water sources,
the Pripyat River joins
at the place
where Chernobyl lies.
On the map showing the areas contaminated by Caesium 137,
around a third of the river upstream was colored,
meaning that bitter water was pushed into the river.
Within an area ten kilometers around Chernobyl,
under the earthen mounds where wormwood thickly grows,
under the eight hundred earthen mounds,
polluted materials are buried.
Eight hundred earthen mounds turn
underground water into bitter water.
They say that
the sarcophagus has started to crack.
They say that
the condition of the ground is critical
due to the heat and weight.
From the man-made pond of the nuclear power plant,
water flows into the Pripyat River,
the Pripyat flows into the Dnieper,
and the water-rich Dnieper flows
with the bitter water itself.

In "The Flow of Bitter Water," we are made to re-realize how horrible it is that nuclear power plant accidents continue to contaminate rivers and groundwater, and the contamination lasts hundreds of thousands of years. Wakamatsu saw a junction of two rivers near Chernobyl, and he may have imagined contaminant flowing from the eight hundred earthen mounds where it was buried. His power of imagination tells us what would happen to the forest and river if there were an accident at the Fukushima nuclear power plants. (It happened seventeen years later.)

In the poem "A Water Planet Sleeping in a White Aqua," Wakamatsu

prays in the light of a white night, which he saw on the plane via Moscow.

> My lonely flight to the East,
> left Moscow at eight p.m.
> With the sun on the left,
> it feels like time has stopped,
> like I'm floating.
> Here, we have a white night,
> and the setting sun starts to shed the morning sunlight
> at the same time.
> I imagine a river running
> on the surface of the earth
> on a dark stagnant night.
> I imagine
> people sinking into sleep for a brief time
> before the night breaks.
> I wonder
> if butterflies are dancing in their dreams.
> No butterflies
> outside the window.

Wakamatsu may have seen the white night over the sky of Siberia at midnight and remembered the people he met in Chernobyl, Kyiv, Ukraine, and Belarus. I suppose he wished that the butterfly with an "inner life" that Tokoku Kitamura advocated might live forever in the people living with the "bitter water" of the Dnieper River and the Pripyat River.

In the concluding "Epilogue: A Shape of Sorrow," Wakamatsu finishes his series of poems with his thought about children in Ukraine.

> Seeing the statue of Nikko Bosatu (Bodhisattva)
> I thought of the children in Ukraine.
> I realized, late, that
> there is no difference between
> grief 1,000 years ago
> and grief today.

What we experienced in the past
will be scheduled in the future.
Tears overflow my eyes.
Water overflows the Dnieper River.
The bitter water overflows the dam of the Dnieper River.

Nikko Bosatu said to punish dark evil at the bottom of various sufferings by a thousand lights. Wakamatsu's funeral was carried out with no religious faith, respecting his will. He was open to saying that he has no religious belief, influenced by his grandfather. However, reading this epilogue, I felt his love for Ukrainian children and his deep understanding of the religious spirit that produced the Buddha statue as a savior soothing the suffering of unhappy people.

I feel that Wakamatsu's spirit is similar to that of Kenji Miyazawa, a poet of his prefecture, Iwate, who wrote poems and fairytales wishing for children's happiness. For a long time, he taught Kokugo (Japanese) as a high school teacher and recommended books to students as the teacher in charge of the school library. I heard from the people who knew him that he was known among children as a teacher they could consult when they had worries and could not consult with their parents or other teachers. I believe that these eleven poems in *Land of Sorrow* were written by wishing for the happiness of children in such a sorrowful future. For Wakamatsu, true prophecy or prophetic words are the ones that keep children away from unhappiness and save "Captives," the ones that are full of true love from adults.

It seems that the poems of *Land of Sorrow* have not yet been read by many people. To deepen your understanding of the poems, I'd recommend you refer to "Kyiv/Moscow May 18, 1994," "There, Many Rivers Run" and "Night Planet: Three Poems" in The Third Volume, *Critical Essays and Other Writings*. Reading all the *Three Volumes of the Jotaro Wakamatsu Collection* may need time and effort, so I'd recommend you start with these eleven poems in *Land of Sorrow*. If you can understand these representative poems, you can appreciate other poems and critical essays more deeply.

Part 2:
15 Selected Poems

Translated by Naoshi Koriyama

Woods at Night I

Woods are your pubic hair.
Low on the horizon, woods remain stagnant in love.
The trees place their branches one on top of the other.
Woods at night.
Animals keep hiding themselves,
looking up at the stars through the trees,
sniffing each other's smell.
I wonder if it will rain soon.
Stars are flickering ceaselessly.
A sudden gust of wind.
Trees' branches bend.
Trees themselves bend.
The woods bend.
The night bends.
Oh, you, my beloved woman!
Let's act like animals,
spending the night in the cave of the woods, projecting ourselves
    onto the stars.
Let's sniff the smell of each other's body.
What we hoped to get always turned out to be different from what
    we got.
We have been always betrayed by the different thing.
We were afraid of the myth, and we endlessly looked for another
    thing.
What is "another, different thing" for us?

We burn your smell.
We burn my smell.
Our smells spread all over the woods,
and we pick up stars.
What was that white thing that flashed across the retina?
Was it my spirit or my body?
Was it your spirit or your body?
Was it the spirit or body of someone dead?
Would it be something different from what we looked for?
The woods bend.
The night bends.
Love bends.
Oh, you, my beloved woman!
Let's act at least like animals
and burn our smells.

A sudden gust of wind.
To the woods of night low on the horizon
a rainy season comes.

Woods at Night IV

When the sixteenth nuclear bomb test was conducted in America in 1957, a "nerve test" was conducted at the same time.

The Observation Post that announces the passing of time stands
  black, indicating its mercilessness.

Nevada, September 2, 1957

I don't care
whether they call me "Joe"
or "Tommy."
We belong
to the honorable 82nd Airborne Corps,
under the direct command of Captain Storebell. We
cannot be anything but that.
It would be God's will.

    Woods all around
    conceal themselves in black,
    slightly swaying,
    caused by the breathing of the beasts.
    The time, 5 a.m.,
    has long passed.

However,
however,

coming nearer to the morning is
going farther away from the morning.
Isn't coming nearer to God
going farther away from God?

A white beast has flown by.
What was that?
From where to where did it fly?
Was it God's will
in the same way?

It's quite dark, isn't it?

Can the length of 4,400 meters
from the epicenter
ever be a distance that can give us peace of mind
or
comfort?

It was the instinct
that sent the white beast flying
to distant mountains.
Ah, let's throw away our instinct, too.

At this dawn
woods retreat
into night.

It's dark like your eyes, isn't it?

Nothing would ever exist
before us,
no trenches,
no concrete walls,
no steel roofs,
and
even God
wouldn't exist
around us.

No birds ever fly.
Clouds are torn up.
The blinking stars wander
low like my intention,
shattered.
Even beasts wouldn't walk forward.

It's not dark.
It's light, isn't it?
You should say, "It's light,"
In such a time as this.

The one who stands at the gallows would go up, counting the steps:
13......12......11......
10 seconds before......
He moistens his lips with his tongue.

He clears his throat.
Someone mutters,
"A death sentence is pronounced,"
in a trembling voice.
Or rather is it my ears
that are trembling?
Or is it the lips or ears of the world that are trembling?
In the woods of night, nothing is certain.

The ones that announce the passage of time are our
judge,
prison chaplain,
executioner.
Even time is not certain,
neither life nor death.

Execution? No!
Suicide? No!
It's a duel.
Standing, with each other's backs touching, then, we walk forward.
My thinking wanders low
between Life and Death
and,
and,
where is my opponent for the duel......?

......8......7......

Even the distant howl of the coyote is sucked up into the sky,
  no longer heard.

I curl up my body,
placing my head between my knees,
taking a futile defense position like a wood louse.
My hands get tense with extra power, and the sand I held falls
  down.

I don't care
whether they call me "Joe"
or "Tommy,"
as if I were no worthier
than an insect.

Nothing
is around us.
Nothing
is before us.
Nothing whatsoever!

Nothingness.
My father used to say,
"Existence comes out of Nothingness."
What is that
which arises
somewhere,
out of my...

my heart.
And is it trembling?
What is that?
Is it fear?
Or an entreaty?
Or a revolt?

......2......1
I am
0.

Small Poems Longing for Home
Variations following Kenji Miyazawa

1. Mizusawa

The field seems to expand as far as the clouds over there.
Is Mizusawa somewhere over there?
I wonder where your home is.
　　　　—"The Gorin Pass," 2nd Edition of *Spring and Asura*

Thinking that Mizusawa must be somewhere over there,
I look back over the vast Kitakami Plain
at the ridgeway of Mt. Yakeishi.
The Taneyama Heights and the Gorin Pass are on the yonder side.
From this side, we look at the view
which Kenji had looked at from the other side.
Where is your place, I wonder.
The vast expanse of Hitakami Plains—
They ploughed farms.
They drew water into paddy fields.
They set their horses free in the fields.
They chased beasts in the woods.
It was a paradise for the disobedient tribal groups.
If the place over there is Mizusawa,
the river over there must be the Koromo River.
The town over there must be Hiraizumi.
The various views of lands and rivers indicate a Land of Fertility.
Villages float like islands.

They look like an archipelago as far as the clouds over there.
The smoke of burning fields rises in the province of Hitakami.
It is a signal fire giving a message for us, 1,500 years later.

2. Hitokabe Town

> The morning sun shines on the snow and the woods.
> The long town between the hills is shining unusually bright.
> —"Hitokabe Town," 2nd Edition of *Spring and Asura*

At the end of the long town between the hills
there was a liquor store two doors down from the corner that leads
  to the suspension bridge over the Naruse River.
And on the bookshelves of the liquor store there were back num-
  bers of *The Baseball World*.
The baseball team of the long-shaped town between the hills was
  the Naruse Club.
My uncle, too, was a member of the Naruse Club,
and they used to come to our town fifteen kilometers downstream
  to play a game.
We, small boys who were playing with handmade balls made with
  marbles or royal ferns tightly bound with wool, admired their play.
I remember the bus that ran on charcoal gas climbed up the steep
  uphill road, gasping.
Now it is strange that there are no steep slopes on the road to
  Hitokabe Town.
Behind the liquor store flows the Naruse River.
Char fish and daces were swimming, their scales glistening in the

shallows.

The roasted fish on the skewers smelled good.

The liquor store was the home where my mother was raised,
and it's also the home where I was born.

There is a legend handed down in the long town between the hills.

The legend says that there was a boy about 15 or 16 in the tribe of
the "Bad Road King," the chief of the Emishi people.

It is said that the boy hid himself from the royalist army attacking
the Emishi people in a cave on Mt. Omori.

They say that Hitokabemaru, who was hit on the neck, was
handsome.

Am I a descendant of the "Bad Road King"?

Or am I a descendant of the villager who sheltered Hitokabemaru?

There was a fast waterway by the street of the long town between
the hills,
and I once missed my foot, trying to catch a ball, and fell down.

When my face came up above the water, while being swept along,
an arrow shot by the royalist troop flashed by.

3. The Kitakami River

"The Kitakami River carries along a bright air.
The mountain holds its noontime thoughts up high."
—"The Kitakami River Carries along a Bright Air,"
2nd Edition of *Spring and Asura*

The Kitakami River flows on, keeping the light of one thousand
years ago on its surface.

I used to commute to the high school eight kilometers away, cross-
ing a bridge.
I would stop my bicycle by the Sakuragi Bridge, enjoying the wind
blowing over the river.
The trees along the riverbank sway in the wind over the river.
There is something passing by like a wind.
Is that the guy?
If I stand on the bridge, the place seems to be the center of the
entire Universe.
You can also see Mt. Iwate and Mt. Hayachine, small in the distance.
Mt. Tane and the Ubaishi Heights to the east,
Mt. Yakeishi and Mt. Koma to the west,
the old site of the Isawa Castle on the terrace a little upstream,
Atoroi a little downstream,
which is said to have been the ancient base of Aterui, the chief of
the Yezo people.
Aterui became the sacrifice brought over a long distance.
The head that was hit stared at the evening glow in the street of the
capital city.
There is something passing like a wind.
Is that the guy?
Who is "the guy"?
When I stand on the bridge, the present time seems to be the cen-
ter of Eternity.
The Kitakami River flows on, keeping the light of one thousand
years ago on its surface.

For Me, Who Has Already Died

For the Photograph: "At the crematory in Nagasaki" by Joe O'Donnell'

It's me.
The moment I saw the photo,
I knew that it was me,
a fourth-grader in elementary school.

The boy is looking straight ahead,
his lips firmly set,
the hair of his head close-cropped,
his fingers all straightened,
his middle fingers placed along the seams of his knee pants on
    both sides,
his bare heels placed together,
the tips of his feet set apart.
He is surely in the posture of "Attention"
in which we had all been sternly trained,
but the upper part of his body leans forward, just a bit.
His back is somewhat bent
in the posture of "bowing."
In the posture of "bowing," he is carrying his little brother.
The boy is carrying his little brother on his back,
securely tied to his back with a band.
His little brother's head dangles backward.
His little brother is already dead on his back.

Did you see the eyes of the boy carrying his dead little brother on
    his back?
Did you see the eyes of the boy enduring his sorrows?
His eyes are set forward, enduring his sorrows.
What are his eyes looking at, enduring his sorrows?
To what is he "bowing"?

The Earth is overflowing with deaths.
Life and Death are mixed together.
Life and Death are sitting together, touching each other's back,
the big brother and the little brother,
Life and Death separated only by a sheet of cloth.
Death wouldn't be able to notice His own mistake,
even if the life and death of the two brothers were reversed.

The Earth is overflowing with deaths,
dead people are folded and piled up,
and they are swallowed up by the flames of cremation.
A flame shines on the boy's cheeks.
His "bowing" is his final farewell to the numerous dead
who might have been his father, mother, brother, friends,
or even himself.
A farewell from someone who has just barely escaped death.

The boy unties the band,
releases his little brother from his back,
and then
entrusts his little brother who is burning in flames,

the dead person who could have been himself,
to the Memories, enduring his sorrows.

"It's me.
It's a photograph of me, at 10 years old."
The one who was just barely able to remain alive
returns a greeting to me, the dead person in the photograph.
Returning the greeting,
now, a half century later,
now, when a new century has set in,
the boy's sorrows still exist in the reality of Earth.

Japan in a Suitcase, A Collection of Photographs by Joe O'Donnell, (Shogakukan, 1995), p. 97. A photograph of Nagasaki after the war, in 1945. It is a photograph of a boy about 10 years old, carrying his little brother dead on his back to the crematorium which had been temporarily made on a riverbank.

On the Other Side of the Fog and on This Side

1. The Sky Over Zelazowa Wola

I wait, sitting on the bench in the shade.
I see horse chestnut trees,
black locusts,
baby roses.
The breezes that come, dancing through the flowers, feel good
on my cheeks.

The down of poplars is flying through Europe in May.
From the sky over the Ukrainian Plains, too,
the summer's snow is flying, carrying the tiny seeds
toward Krakow and Prague,
toward Belgrade and Sarajevo,
to the garden of the house with white walls covered with ivy where
    Chopin was born,
to the garden of a small concert hall too.

The pianist is Alexander Gavryluk,
a young man about the age of Chopin when he left his homeland,
an exceptionally talented person from the neighboring country,
    Ukraine.
The first concert program is "Fantasia in F minor," opus 49.
Yoshinao Nakada seems to have borrowed its main melody
for his song "Snow is Falling on the Town."
The sky in May is blue,

and the down of poplars, not snow, is flying
over Zelazowa Wola Village in the suburbs of Warsaw.

As if it were joining the concert,
the singing of the skylark comes from the height of the sky.
Browning would say, "The lark's on the wing,"*
while Bin Ueda would say, "A soaring skylark announcing itself,"
and bring it to its end by singing:
"God's in his heaven......
All's right with the world!"
And now, "All's right here," really.

From different parts of Europe,
various people have come, each following their own wish.
People from Korea and Japan, too, have come,
each carrying their own wish,
listening to the "ballad,"
enjoying a "scherzo."
A man walking his dog goes across the yard.
People seem to exist in an extraordinary life, away from their everyday life,
their everyday life mixed with their extraordinary life,
showing something like the substantiveness of everyday life,
and as if considering the "polonaise" to be background music,
a girl, riding a bicycle, passes by the front yard.

Really, "all's right," here now,
but it may be so at this place at this very moment only.

We may be looking at a mere vision,
the piano music being played now too may be just an auditory
   hallucination,
trustworthy things may be only like
the wind that has come, playing through the flowers,
or the down of the poplars that has come, drifting through the
   blue sky of May.

*From "Pippa Passes" by Robert Browning. It's translated as "The Spring Morning" in the book *Kaicho-on* by Bin Ueda.

The Day When a South Wind Blows

1.
The wind blowing from the south
along the shore feels good.
The heads of the surfers waiting for the waves in the open sea appear on and off.
It is the shore of Kitaizumi, Haramachi City, Fukushima Prefecture.
It is 25 kilometers north of the First Nuclear Power Plant of Fukushima.
It is well within the area of the Chernobyl nuclear accident,
where 135,000 inhabitants left in an emergency evacuation.

For instance,
in June 1978,
pinkish spots appeared on the flower petals of spiderworts
in the garden of Mr. Takashi Masukura,
in Minamitanashio, Namie Town, Futaba County, Fukushima Prefecture,
eight kilometers north of the First Plant of the Fukushima Nuclear Electric Power Plant,
but it was concluded that nothing was found that would indicate any relationship
with the operation of the Nuclear Electric Power Plant.

For instance,
a report issued in January of 1980 states:
Cobalt 60 was detected in the sand of the seashore, in Sakhalin

surf clams,
and in sea potatoes at a spot eight hundred meters from the south
    drainage gate
of the First Nuclear Electric Power Reactor
of the First Fukushima Nuclear Electric Power Plant.

For instance,
data gathered in June 1980:
Cobalt 60 was detected from the air of a primary school's playground
at Kiyohashi, Namie Town, Futaba County, Fukushima Prefecture,
which was eight kilometers north of the First Fukushima Nuclear
    Electric Power Plant.

For instance,
in September 1988,
the hair on my head and body fell off all at once
in Sakae Town, Haramachi City, Fukushima Prefecture,
which was twenty-five kilometers north of the First Fukushima
    Nuclear Power Plant.
When I washed my hair one time, the hair that fell off filled a rice
    bowl.
Of course,
they will not admit a relationship between the falling off of my hair
and the operation of the nuclear electric power reactor, but…

The wind blowing from the south feels good.
Far out in the open sea, away from the surfers drifting in the waves,
two ferries slowly come closer from right and left and then part

from each other.
I can see the time which seems so overwhelming.
Sounds of the world have gone.
All's right with the world,
or
do we see what is coming?

2.
On November 2, 1978,
eight years before the Chernobyl nuclear disaster,
in the third reactor of the First Nuclear Electric Power Plant of
  Fukushima,
five reactor control rods fell off during a hydraulic test of the pressure vessel,
and the critical state lasted as long as 7 hours and 30 minutes,
the first time in Japan.
The Tokyo Electric Power Company finally admitted the accident
in March 2007 after the passage of 29 years.

In another case,
on October 21, 1984,
the second nuclear power reactor of the First Nuclear Electric
  Power Plant
of Fukushima made an emergency stop due to a critical state
during a pressure tolerance test,
the cover-up of which the Tokyo Electric Power Company finally
  admitted
in March 2007, 23 years later.

Reactor control rod malfunctions occurred in Fukushima as follows:

February 12, 1979: 5th Reactor of the First Nuclear Electric Power Plant.

September 10, 1980: 2nd Reactor of the First Nuclear Electric Power Plant.

June 15, 1993: 3rd Reactor of the Second Nuclear Electric Power Plant.

February 22, 1998: 4th Reactor of the First Nuclear Electric Power Plant.

All these accidents had been concealed until March 2007,

then, they were finally revealed at the meeting of the Federation of Electric Power Companies in the Keidanren Building, Ohtemachi, Chiyoda-ku, Tokyo,

which is as far away as two hundred kilometers south-southwest from the First Nuclear Power Electric Company of Fukushima.

In November 2007,

off Kitaizumi Shore, Minamisōma City, Fukushima Prefecture,

which is twenty-five kilometers north of the First Nuclear Electric Power Plant,

neither surfers nor ferries are seen,

the sounds of the world are gone,

the winds coming from the south touch my skin.

What is that which we see?

The Town Has Melted Down

1.

rice stores, vegetable stores, fish dealers, tofu stores, miso & soy sauce stores, pickle shops, steamed adzuki-bean jelly shops, rice cracker shops, candy stores, old-fashioned penny candy stores, liquor stores, oil shops, milk shops, ice shops, household goods stores, charcoal stores, brown coal dealers, apparel stores, haberdasheries, tailors, weavers, net dealers, dyehouses, laundries, stationery shops, bookstores, watchmakers, photograph shops, printers, newspaper shops, drug stores, hospitals, midwives, barbershops, hairdressers, clog shops, shoe stores, flower shops, artificial flower makers, leaf-metal dealers, metal workers, dealers of Buddhist altar articles, temples, churches, hotels, restaurants, diners, playhouses, bait and tackle stores, post offices, banks, credit unions, pawn shops, bus companies, transport companies, livery stables, horse dealers, handymen, lumber dealers, woodworking shops, cabinet-makers, joiners, tatami makers, futon stores, master carpenters, tile makers, galvanized sheet iron craftsmen, tinsmiths, hardware dealers, casters, pots and kettles stores, menders of pots and pans, dealers of farm tools, farriers

2.
About 10,000 people lived in the town where I grew up.
I could walk from one end of the town to the other in 15 minutes.
Various stores lined up tightly side by side.
Various craftsmen worked in front of the stores.
Most of the things necessary for living were obtainable in the town.

The relationships of people helping each other must have been well established.
Handicapped people too had their work,
and it was not a closed community, but open to outsiders.
Just like a popular culture which developed in the "cities" of Europe,
citizens' culture was being brought about in the small local cities of Japan
from the end of the Edo period* to the beginning of the Shōwa period.*

And it was the 100,000,000 All Nation Mobilization System that destroyed the workings
of such local towns.
Such things as the National Defense System, Neighborhood Network,
and the Women's Patriotic Association destroyed the workings of the town I grew up in.

*The Edo period (1603-1867)
*The Shōwa period (1926-1989)

3.
Odaka Town, Sōma County, Fukushima Prefecture, was small-sized
and it was very similar to the town where I grew up.
There was a waterway in the center of the straight Old Highway,
which symbolized the relationships of the people supporting each other.

In the neighborhood where "Kuson," Shozo Omagari, lived,
there lived "Yosei," Yoshio Suzuki, who was five years older,
and "Fuko," Takaaki Hara, who was one year younger.*
They formed a haiku group, which they called the "Bitter Tea Club,"
in which they tried to improve each other's skills in haiku.
At his own expense, Shozo published the "posthumous manu-
scripts" of Yoshio, who passed away young.
When Shozo was working hard, compiling the "Senryu Glossary"
and suffering from poverty,
Takaaki helped him in every way possible.
When Shozo died, Yoshio's son, Yasuzo, wrote a eulogy, "Reminiscences
about Kuson," for him.
Takaaki erected a tombstone for Shozo in the cemetery of his own
family, comforting his soul.
Yoshie Hirata and Yasuzo Suzuki, who was two years younger,
both attended
Sōma Middle School and the Second High School of the prewar
education system,
each of them respecting and encouraging the other.
Yoshie translated *What Should We Do?* by Lenin and edited *Lectures
on the History of the Development of Capitalism in Japan.*
Yasuzo wrote *A Historical Study of the Constitution* and had *An
Outline of the Draft of the Constitution* published.

It was the 100,000,000 All Nation Mobilization System that destroyed the workings
of local small towns which were bringing about a citizens' culture.
Such systems as Universal Conscription, the Neighborhood Network

and the Women's Patriotic Association destroyed the workings of
   the town,
which had raised "Kuson" Omagari and Yasuzo Suzuki.

*Translator's note: "Kuson," "Yosei" and "Fuko" are the pen names they used
among themselves in their haiku club.

4.
In the local small towns where the setup of people supporting each
   other's lives somehow managed to remain,
large-sized stores came in, invading from America,
and small stores closed their doors one after another.
Tofu stores stopped making tofu,
vegetable stores closed their doors,
craftsmen left their tailors' shops.
More and more stores kept their shutters pulled down in the town.

When a larger supermarket opened in the suburbs,
large stores in town withdrew promptly.
People walking in the street have disappeared.
Streets are used only by cars,
and the town has lost its function as a town.

5.
When the nuclear power station which had been brought from
   America exploded,
Odaka Town which was 15 kilometers from the nuclear power
   station was designated as "Alerted Zone."

It didn't only mean that the people in the town should be on an
    alert,
but it was a directive that the people in the town should take ref-
    uge in some other places.
It was a directive that the people there should get out of the place.
With the meltdown of the nuclear power station,
a town which can be found in any local area has melted down
and several towns around have become places where no people can live.
The town was no longer an ordinary town.

Unreasonable Deaths Occur Continually

Although the country was not at war, towns and villages collapsed.
If it were a natural disaster, we could accept it with resignation.
No, even if it were a natural disaster, we couldn't accept it with
  resignation,
but the disaster deprived people of their reason for living and of
  their future.

On April 12, 2011, Iidate Village of Sōma County, Fukushima Prefecture,
was designated a "Planned Evacuation Zone," and on the following morning,
the oldest man in the village dressed up neatly and took his own
  life at age 102,
saying, "I have lived too long. I don't want to leave this place."

On June 11, 2011, at Tamano, Sōma City, Fukushima Prefecture,
a 54-year-old dairyman who had 40 milk cows took his own life in
  his manure hut,
because he was not able to bear the anguish of discarding the milk,
which he could not ship.
"Dairymen
had their hands and legs wrenched off
by nuclear power generation."

On June 22, 2011, at Haramachi-ku, Minamisōma City, Fukushima
  Prefecture,

a 93-year-old woman who used to live alone, occasionally separated from her family, took her own life in the yard,
leaving four suicide notes, which read, "Goodbye. I will seek refuge in the tomb."

On July 1, 2011, at Yamakiya, Kawamata Town, Date County,
Fukushima Prefecture,
a 58-year-old unemployed woman, who had temporarily returned
to her home in the "Planned Evacuation Zone,"
set herself on fire in a vacant lot,
saying, "I wouldn't like to seek refuge. I'd like to live as before."

On May 28, 2012, at Namie Town, Futaba County, Fukushima
Prefecture,
one year and two months after the area had been designated
a "Restricted Zone," a 62-year-old storekeeper,
who had temporarily returned to his home, killed himself in his
storeroom,
thinking, "I may no longer go back to my ordinary life."

Even if the families of the deceased file a case against the Tokyo
Electric Power Company,
it will be rejected with the excuse that the cause-and-effect relationship can't be established.
Suicides never cease to happen among those who have had their
reason for living taken away.
Unreasonable deaths never cease to occur in this country, though
it is not at war.

Revolts of Uncivilized Tribes

In ancient times, there was a view that held: "China is the center."
People thought they were at the center, controlling the world,
considering the districts around them "uncivilized,"
looking down on the inhabitants there, calling the people around
them
Eastern Barbarians, Western Beasts, Southern Savages, or Northern
Primitives.

The "self-centered view" spread as far as the islands in the Eastern Seas.
The royal power of Yamato called the native inhabitants
in the eastern and northern districts Iteki, Emishi, or Kazoku,
trying to subjugate them,
and treated them differently,
calling them Ifu or Fushu according to the level of their adaptation.

Naturally, resistant activities occurred frequently.
For instance, revolts occurred in the 770s, as follows:
In 770, the Emishi people revolted and ran away back to remoter
areas.
In 774, the Emishi people revolted, invading the Monou Castle.
In 776, the Emishi people of Shiwa and Isawa revolted.
In 777, the Kazoku people revolted, defeating the troops of Dewa.*

Toward the end of the Nara period,* there lived a county mayor,
Koreharinokimi Azamaro in Iji County, Mutsu Province,

who was a descendant of the Ifu tribe.
The name, Azamaro, reminds us of a man of imposing features.
In 780, he revolted in the Korehari Castle and repelled Kino
    Hirozumi, the administrator, and his followers,
and he invaded the Taga Castle a few days later.

It was nine years after the Revolt of Houki
that Tamonokimi Aterui repelled
the expeditionary force of the Yamato Royal Authority
in the Battle of Subuse in Isawa in 789.
Like Azamaro or Aterui, countless rebels have faded
into the yonder side of memories
without being recorded in history.

*Translator's note: Dewa roughly covered the present-day Yamagata and Akita
Prefectures.
*Translator's note: the Nara period (710-794)

Native People Have Something to Say to Yamato, Japan

One of the policemen who was dispatched from Japan
threw the words, "You, natives! You, savages!"
at the Uchinanchu* protesting against the construction of a U.S. base.

If Uchinanchu are natives,
we, too, are natives.
That's right. We, too, are indigenous human beings.
Ever since I was born, I have never lived south of Shirakawa.
I'm "a native of the Northeast," "a local barbarian."

In the world of the electric power industry,
people used to say, "How lucky the Tokyo Electric Power Company is!
They have many colonies."
The Tokyo Electric Power Company set up nuclear power plants
in all their "colonies."
Eventually, nuclear disasters broke out,
depriving local people of their lives and their ways of living.

It is said that in every place where children evacuated to from
   Fukushima,
they were bullied and called "You, germ!"
My advice to the child who is bullied is:
Say to the bully, "If you don't like germs, you don't eat bread and
   natto, do you?"

"If radiation is contagious, ask your parents
to oppose the operation of the Nuclear Electric Power Plants
in Hamaoka or Tokai, which are closer and more dangerous than
    Fukushima."

By the Japan-U.S. Security Treaty of 1951,
Okinawa was put under U.S. Military Administration for as long
    as twenty years,
U.S. bases have been closely built,
even after the reversion of Okinawa to Japan,
U.S. military personnel are given extraterritorial rights
just as in the time of occupation.
Our "country" has not exercised its sovereignty faithfully,
approving of the present circumstances just like a colony.
The lives and ways of living of the local inhabitants have been
    ignored.

Beware! You, Yamato people, who are mistreating the "natives of
    the colony"!
Isn't the whole land that you call "our country" a colony?
The anger of those people living in the twofold colony has passed
    its limits.
Take away all the U.S. military bases!
Decommission all the nuclear power plants!

*Editor's Note: Uchinanchu refers to the people of Okinawa.

Richness of the Heart

There is a bold, creative power.
There is something that resounds in our hearts.
Why, indeed?
In spite of the fact that they were created several thousand years ago?

A feeling of a fertile human life can be felt.
There is a real feeling of a human body.
Why, indeed?
In spite of the fact that they have been buried under the ground
   for several thousand years?

I can feel that my thoughts might have been included in them.
I can feel a strong feeling of intimacy.
Why, indeed?
In spite of the fact that we have been out of touch for several thou-
   sand years?

What is our Age in history like?
What have we done?
What kind of time have we spent?

What is our Age in history like?
Or, is our Age after the time of the atomic bombing of Hiroshima?
Or, is it after the collapse of the Soviet Union?
Or, should we assume it to be a much longer period of time?

What have we done
in the period of 500 years or 250 years
after the Renaissance or the Age of Discovery,
after the Reformation, the People's Revolution, or the Industrial
   Revolution?

What is our Age really like?
Since the time when Buddha was born?
Since the time when Confucius passed away?
Since the time when Pericles advocated for a democratic
   government?

Does what we call "Our Age" mean
the last 2,500 years,
even if it may be impossible to trace back to the time before that?

But the fact that we have repeated
reforms or revolutions
may signify that there have been reactions each time.
Are we really unmanageable animals?

During the time of more than a hundred years
wars have become epoch-makers.
No matter in whatever favorable light we may look at ourselves.
We must be unmanageable animals.

We have used atomic bombs.

We have been using electricity produced by nuclear power.
We have been killing each other, a whole country against another.

If there ever is an age that would follow ours,
have we been creating something we can be proud of
and leave to the following age?
We cannot help but leave something desolate, don't you think?

On these islands, Jōmon people* had been living
for a long period of time, more than 10,000 years,
till about the same time as Pericles lived
in ancient Greece.

We may not be able to say that in the period when the Jōmon
    people were living
they were blessed with a good living environment,
but we can imagine that they had a fertile way of life.

Though we were overwhelmed by the originality of their earthen-
    ware vessels with a flame-shaped rim,
we can feel the warmth of human beings.
Where did they ever obtain it?
They must have obtained it out of their hearts.

Earthenware with human faces, earthenware with human figures,
    light-resistant clay dolls,
clay dolls with their hands held behind their back, a laughing clay
    figure,

a clay figure of a pregnant woman, a clay figure holding a child, children's handprints or footprints, clay human faces.

We can see the fertility of their hearts.
Where else can we have anything as attractive as these?

*Translator's note: Jōmon people: Ancient Japanese people who lived in the Jōmon period, who produced straw-rope patterned pottery.

A Message to the Future, 3,000 Years from Now

More than two hundred Japanese walnuts from the latter part of
    the Jōmon period,
which are said to have been tightly packed in a woven bamboo basket
and stored 3,000 years ago,
have been found in the ruins at Sagiuchi of Kashima, Minamisōma
    City.

The information board of the Sagiuchi Inari Shrine adjoining the
    site says:
"This is the Land of a Mild Winter and Clear Water."
This area has been blessed with a fertile natural environment
as flood plains of the Mano River and the Kamimano River,
and chestnuts trees, Japanese horse chestnuts, and walnuts must
    have been growing abundantly in the wild.
The clear underground water delivered the message of the people
    who had begun to settle down here after the passage of 3,000 years.

The town where I lived in my childhood is another town,
but on the riverbank behind my grandparents' home there grew
    walnut trees,
and chestnut trees grew in the mountain where farms were.
We enjoyed picking up the nuts,
thinking of the life of the Jōmon people.

The Jōmon People knew where tsunamis couldn't reach.

No tsunami would come up to Sagiuchi, nor to the Urajiri Shell
   Mound of Odaka.
The Urajiri Shell Mound had been a good, luxurious dinner table
   throughout the Jōmon period,
serving littleneck clams, corbicula clams, wild duck, deer, wild boar,
sea bass, gobies, sardines, sea breams, eels, and carp.

When the Man'yo period* came in, the Yamato people ruled the land.
The area was named "Mano," and "Grassy Field of Mano" became
   a favorite placename often sung in Japanese poetry.
If we look at a map made forty years ago,
we can see many marks of paddy fields and mulberry fields around
   Sagiuchi,
and we can see an image of an affluent farm village.
But now, almost all the paddy fields are gone, not to mention the
   mulberry fields.
The area has become a residential district for those people
who had been hit by nuclear accidents and lost their homes and
   way of life and had to take refuge.
Many of the people have given up all hope of going back to their
   homes.

What kind of message are we going to give
to the people 3,000 years from now?

*The Man'yo period: the latter part of the 7ᵗʰ century, when poems in the
Man'yo Shu were written.

No Armaments Are Necessary

I will make the year of my birth the starting point.
If I go back seventy years, it is 1865, the first year of the Keiou
  period.
The closing days of the Tokugawa government, which I thought
  were in the long past,
are unexpectedly close.
If I go back eighty years, it's 1855, the third year of the Ansei
  period.
European countries sent their fleets, demanding that Japan open
  its doors to the world.
But Japan had no armaments strong enough for a war at that time.
I cannot help thinking that it was fortunate for Japan.

After that, Japan forced itself to build up stronger armaments.
Its first attempt at war was dispatching troops to Taiwan in 1874,
  the seventh year of the Meiji period.
Japan kept fighting wars for seventy years.
Many people of other countries were victimized.
Many people of Japan too were victimized in the wars.

This organization called a "nation" treated its people as mere objects.
The age in which I have lived has disregarded the dignity of human life.
In 1937, two years after my birth,
the bombers of Germany attacked Guernica of Spain.
Japanese troops killed even ordinary civilians in Nanking, China.

The age of indiscriminate mass murder had begun.
In firearms, a machine-gun was made out of a single-shot gun.
Cannon balls of large-caliber artillery and large-scale bombs were used.
Flamethrowers, incendiary bombs and poison gas destroyed
    human lives.
Even a nuclear explosion was turned into a medium of mass
    slaughter and mass destruction.
This organization called a "nation" even used human beings as
    weapons,
human bombs, human torpedoes, special attack planes, total
    deaths of entire fighting units.

Even now, seventy years since 1945,
such things as the nations, ideologies and religions
that human beings have made
keep dividing them into groups by using one pretext or another.
Human beings are being treated as tools.

When we think of all the foolish things which human beings have done
in the one hundred years since the First World War,
we can feel proud of the seventy years during which Japan hasn't
    had a war.
We have been fortunate that we haven't had armaments strong
    enough to fight a war.
But the period of seventy years has made us forget our memories,
made us forget the foolishness of having armaments strong enough
    to go to war.

Human Beings Have Speech

We have no trouble finding a place to live,
living an amiable life with family members,
and we exchange greetings when we meet neighbors.

We have no trouble getting something to eat.
We have no trouble getting something to wear.
We can go anywhere we want to go.
We can do what we want to do,
and we can say what we want to say.

If we are free to do these things,
we should be calm at heart, but…

We know
that there is a girl whose whole body is damaged by broken pieces
    of a cannonball,
there is a boy holding a gun in his hands,
there are people trying to get on a tiny boat
already loaded with refugees far over its waterline,
conflicts are going on endlessly,
and there are people suffering from unreasonable causes now,
and people are dying unreasonable deaths now.
We know these things.

Out of the experiences that I had till my tenth summer,

I pray
that my children and grandchildren will not suffer from unreason-
    able things,
that no people will suffer from unreasonable things.

Human beings can use speech.
Let's stop armed conflicts and solve the conflicts by talking,
so that no person may suffer from unreasonable things,
so that every person may remain calm at heart.

As long as there are people who are suffering from unreasonable
    things,
we cannot be calm at heart.

To My Unknown Young Friends
An Invitation to the Central Library of the City

A human being can become a human being before being born
by being connected first to his or her mother's blood
with the umbilical cord.

Even after being born,
a human being can become a new human being
by being connected with various umbilical cords.

The library is an umbilical cord.
A human being obtains a new life
by being connected with the intellect of various human beings.

A book on the bookshelf,
a book you take in your hands,
which has been waiting for you to take it
may change you into a new human being.

Editor's note: This poem was written by request of the Central Library of
Minamisōma City. It is hand-written on a signature card, and has been framed
and displayed in the library ever since December 2009.

BRIEF PERSONAL HISTORY

Author

Jotaro Wakamatsu (1935~2021). Born in Oshu city, Iwate prefecture. After graduating from Fukushima University, he worked as a Japanese language teacher at high schools in Hama-street in Fukushima prefecture. He lived in Minamisōma city in Fukushima.

Works: *Jotaro Wakamatsu Collection: Three Volumes* (Coal Sack Publishing Company).

Eleven collections of poems such as "Woods at Night" and "Revolts of Uncivilized Tribes." Three collections of essays such as "Fukushima Nuclear Refugees" and "Abandoned People in Nuclear Disasters."

Translators

Keiko Yonaha (1953~). Born in Naha City, Okinawa prefecture. She is a retired professor from Meio University. An interpreter and translator.

Works: *Anger of Okinawa* (collection of essays) *What We See from Okinawa* (collection of poems) *Small World* (English translation of Maya Inoue's poems) All, Coal Sack publishing company.

Naoshi Koriyama (1926~). Born in Kikaijima in Amami, Kagoshima prefecture. He is an emeritus professor at Toyo University and an English translator.

Works: *Attractive Force of a Poet* (Coal Sack publishing company) and "A Fresh Loaf of Poetry from Japan" (English Poems).